RICHARD A. LUPOFF

ANCIENT EVIL RETURNS
And Other Stories

Complete and Unabridged

LINFORD
Leicester

First published in Great Britain

First Linford Edition
published 2018

A catalogue record for this book is available
from the British Library.

ISBN 978–1–4448–3827–5

Published by
F. A. Thorpe (Publishing)
Anstey, Leicestershire

Set by Words & Graphics Ltd.
Anstey, Leicestershire
Printed and bound in Great Britain by
T. J. International Ltd., Padstow, Cornwall

This book is printed on acid-free paper

ANCIENT EVIL RETURNS
& OTHER STORIES

A youthful journalist seeks to unravel the mysterious disaster that struck a New England town nearly a century ago . . . A young couple, stranded by a monstrous storm, seek shelter in a darkened town and discover a dangerous cult . . . A peculiar child is born . . . A young woman and her boyfriend find themselves in terrible danger . . . A brilliant academic begins to make a disquieting discovery . . . These are the problems faced by ordinary people as they encounter extraordinary mysteries when *Ancient Evil Returns*.

Contents

The Doom That Came To Dunwich

When a traveler in north central Massachusetts takes the wrong fork at the junction of the Aylesbury Pike just beyond Dean's Corners, he may feel that he has fallen through a crack in time and emerged into an earlier era in New England. The countryside is marked by rolling hills and meadows, spotted here and there with stands of woodland that, at first glance, appear lush and healthy, but that, upon closer examination, seem to emit an almost palpable miasma of *wrongness*. The grasses are oddly yellow. The tree trunks seem to be writhing in pain, while their leaves appear oddly *fat* and to give off an unpleasantly oily exudation.

If one arrives in what has become known as Dunwich Country at night, the sense of temporal alienation is especially strong. The few advertising billboards that were erected along the Pike in earlier decades have fallen into wrack and ruin, but no one has bothered either to rehabilitate or to remove them. The few tatters of once-colorful posters that remain attached to their frameworks, flapping in every errant gust of wind, remind the traveler of products long removed from the market: Graham-Paige automobiles, Atwater-Kent superheterodyne radio sets, Junius Brutus Cigars.

Even tuning the radio to stations in Boston, Providence or Worcester does little good, for the particular conformation of the terrain, or perhaps the presence of deposits of as yet undetected ores beneath the ground, or of unexplained atmospheric conditions, makes it impossible to receive more than an unpleasant mélange of sound, interspersed with indecipherable whisperings and gurglings.

Rounding the base of Sentinel Hill on the outskirts of Dunwich, the site of the infamous 'horror' of 1928, the traveler beholds an incongruous sight: a modern laboratory and office building of mirrored glass construction. Activity in the building proceeds uninterrupted, day and night. A wire-mesh fence surrounds the facility, and a single rolling gateway is guarded at all times by stern-faced young men and women. These individuals are clad in dark uniforms of unfamiliar cut and tint, identifiable neither as military nor police in nature. Each uniform jacket carries a shoulder patch and each uniform cap a metal device, but the spiraling helix into which these insignia are formed is also unique to the Dunwich facility. This ensign, it may be noted, is laminated as well on the stock of the dull-black, frightening sidearm which each uniformed guard carries.

A small wooden plaque is mounted beside the rolling gate, in sparse letters identifying the facility as the property of the Dunwich Research Project. No newspaper files or directories of government organizations make mention of the Dunwich Research Project, and neither the directory issued by the Dunwich Telephone Company, nor that company's

Directory Assistance operators, are able to furnish a number by means of which the facility may be contacted.

However, careful study of federal appropriations documents of past years may reveal 'black' items in the budgets of major agencies which, a selected few Washington insiders are willing to concede, may indeed have been directed through back channels to the Project. Further study of federal records will show that these covert appropriations for the Dunwich Research Project began in 1929.

The initial appropriation was extremely small, but in later years the funding for the Dunwich Research Project increased despite crisis, Depression, or war. The names of every President from Herbert Hoover to the present time will be found attached to these 'black' items.

It was to this region that young Cordelia Whateley, a graduate student of anthropology at McGill University in Montreal, Quebec, drove her conservative grey four-door sedan in the late spring of the year. Her examinations over for the semester, she had determined to spend the next several months researching her master's dissertation on the events of 1928. It was Miss Whateley's belief that an encounter with one or more alien beings had provided the basis for those horrific happenings. Because she was herself a member of a distant (and undecayed) branch of the Whateley family, she had been inculcated from infancy with a revulsion for her (decayed) kith and kin. This she wished to resolve once and for all: to prove that her distant cousin Wilbur Whateley had been not so much a menace to be feared and loathed as he was a sport of nature deserving of the sympathy and aid which he failed to receive from those around him.

Miss Whateley brought her automobile to a stop outside the rolling gate of the Dunwich Research Project. The guard on duty, a young man with a square jaw and muscular build, approached her and courteously asked her business at the Project. She showed him a letter from her faculty adviser at McGill, addressed to the Director of the Dunwich Institute, and a response, on Institute letterhead, welcoming her inquiry and authorizing all concerned to offer the bearer every possible courtesy and assistance.

The merest suggestion of a smile played around the lips of the guard as he handed the documents back to Miss Whateley.

'You'll want the Dunwich Institute, miss,' the guard explained. 'This is the Dunwich Research Project. The Institute is in Dunwich Town. On South Water Street. Dr. Armitage is the director. That's his signature on the bottom of your letter. You want the Institute, miss. The Research Project is off limits.'

He gestured courteously, suggesting but not exactly duplicating, a military salute. Then, with a series of clear and vigorous hand gestures (he was wearing white gloves) he directed Miss Whateley to depart and return to town.

Cordelia Whateley complied, swinging her automobile around and pointing its nose back toward Dunwich proper. As she circled Sentinel Hill she could not help noticing that an array of radar dishes dotted the top of the hill. To her, they looked like a recrudescence of white, puffy toadstools.

The town of Dunwich had neither grown nor changed noticeably from the illustrations and descriptions Cordelia Whateley had studied in preparation for her visit to the region. Authorities in the United States had been reluctant to send materials dealing with Dunwich out of the country, even to so friendly a neighbor as that to the north, but a friend of Miss Whateley's at the University of Massachusetts had managed to borrow many such documents and share them with the researcher by means of electronic transmission.

As Cordelia Whateley motored down Winthrop Street toward South Water, she noticed that Osborn's Store still stood at the corner of Winthrop and Blindford. Beside it, a grimy-windowed establishment advertised EATS and ALE. No other name identified the establishment, but after a lifetime in which her world had become increasingly dominated by malls and franchise enterprises, Cordelia

Whateley found the survival of Osborn's Store and of an establishment identified solely as EATS and ALE oddly comforting.

Opposite Osborn's Store stood a steepled, greystone building. Cordelia tried to make out the device that topped the steeple. In the darkness she could not be certain, but she thought it was the same ensign she had seen on the uniforms of the guards at the Dunwich Research Project. Lights flickered inside the building, and the sound of chanting could be heard.

She located the Dunwich Institute and stood before its Spartan exterior, searching for a means of admittance. The Institute was located in a building of colonial architecture, but rather than serving as a source of elegance and charm, the frame construction, with its chipped and faded whitewash and its black front door surmounted by a dust-shrouded fanlight, caused a shudder to pass through her body.

Beside the door a rectangular brass plate, once gleaming but now covered with a patina of dullness, still bore the legend, *Dunwich Institute — founded 1928 — Henry Armitage, Ph.D. President*. Cordelia Whateley searched for a doorbell, and, failing to locate one, instead reached for the brass knocker bolted to the wooden door. The knocker, covered with the same dull patina as the plate, was shaped like a creature differing from any Cordelia Whateley had ever before seen. It bore many tentacles, and great staring eyes, and from it there seemed to seep a miasma of pure evil such as she had never in her life encountered.

Cordelia Whateley had taken her large, well-filled purse with her when she left her automobile. Now, having retrieved the purse and clutching it with one hand, she drew a breath, grasped the brass creature, raised it and let it fall. It struck with a loud, metallic sound of unpleasant nature. Cordelia Whateley found herself staring from her hand to the knocker, and then to her hand once again. Surely the knocker was of brass: of old, tarnished brass. Why, then, did her hand feel as if her fingers had grasped the rubbery, slimy, moist tentacles of a living creature? And why, when she released the door-knocker, had it seemed to cling stubbornly to her fingers so that she had to pull them away to gain her release?

She had not long to ponder the problem, for the door drew back noisily on rusted hinges and she stood face to face with an aged individual who blinked at her with faded, rheumy eyes. He stood well over six feet in height. His sparse hair was pure white and his face bore an expression of despair overlaid with chronic fear.

'I am Henry Armitage,' the old man said. 'Who are you, young woman, and what do you want of me?'

Cordelia Whateley was taken aback by the old man's appearance but she had rehearsed for this moment and she delivered the lines she had prepared.

'I — I am Cordelia Whateley. From McGill University. I — I wrote to you about my work, and you sent me this reply.' She held Armitage's own letter so he could see it in the yellow light filtering from behind him. Was it possible? Yes, the Institute building was illuminated by oil-lamp and candle. With a chilling shock she realized that she had not seen an electric appliance or even a gaslight in Dunwich.

Although Cordelia Whateley had arrived in Dunwich Country at an hour when the afternoon sunlight was still fairly bright, here in the narrow streets of the town itself a darkness had descended that was not the comforting, pleasant darkness of a New England evening. Involuntarily, Cordelia Whateley looked behind her. The streets of Dunwich seemed abnormally empty of pedestrian traffic, and the few canvas-covered vehicles that moved on the old streets seemed almost to huddle within themselves as they passed.

Armitage extended a thin hand covered with pale, wrinkled skin. 'Come in. You are late. Almost too late. I receive very few visitors. I expected you earlier in the day.'

Cordelia Whateley followed Armitage into the ancient building. An almost palpable miasma of age and decay seemed to arise from the heavy furnishings and threadbare carpet. Armitage indicated an overstuffed chair covered in faded velvet. Cordelia Whateley lowered herself carefully into it.

'I would have been here earlier,' she tried to explain, 'but — '

'But you went to Sentinel Hill, didn't you?' Armitage cut her off.

'Yes, I — '

'You tried to get into the Project. The Dunwich Research Project. I was afraid of that. You're very lucky indeed.'

'Lucky? I don't understand. I — ' Cordelia Whateley put her hand to her forehead. 'I'm so sorry. Could I have a glass of water? I'm afraid I'm feeling faint.'

While Armitage was out of the room, Cordelia Whateley studied its contents as best she could without leaving her chair. The walls were covered with glass-fronted bookcases, all of them filled to their limits. Many were locked. The books themselves, for the most part, looked ancient. The bindings were tattered; such

12

lettering as Cordelia Whateley could make out was faded. In size, the volumes ranged from huge tomes that would cover a desktop if opened, to tiny items little larger than a common postage stamp.

Her eye was caught in particular by a small book, little more than a pamphlet, in fact, with an illustration on its cover. The illustration, barely visible in the yellow light of the dark, musty room, seemed a crude representation of the door-knocker that Cordelia Whateley had handled at this very building. The slim book was bound in black leather, and its title, embossed in gold lettering in an obsolete typeface, read simply, *De Obéissance à les Maîtres Vieux*.

Henry Armitage's hand on her shoulder startled Cordelia Whateley. She gasped and turned. He extended a glass toward her. It might once have been part of a set of fine crystal but its rim now showed a jagged chip, its sides were streaked and the water it contained was of a vaguely unpleasant color and odor. Cordelia Whateley accepted the vessel and took one reluctant sip of its contents before placing it on a dust-coated table.

'You asked why I thought you lucky,' Armitage said. 'Visitors to the Project sometimes disappear. Young Selena Bishop went up there last spring and hasn't been heard of since. In Dunwich Town, people don't like to receive an invitation to visit the Project.'

'But then,' Cordelia Whateley frowned, 'why do they go? Why don't they just refuse to go?'

'When you're summoned to the Project, you go. That's the way it is in Dunwich Town.'

'But people could just move away, couldn't they? Don't the buses run? And the Aylesbury Pike is nearby. It's only an hour or two to Boston by automobile.'

'You don't leave Dunwich Country as easily as you might think, young miss. No, not if *they* want you to stay here. Rice and Morgan thought they could leave. They learned better. I'm the only one left now, of the three of us. I was the oldest, and you'd think I'd be long gone by now. But Rice was buried at sea and Morgan was cremated. They'd both left instructions that, whatever happened, *they were not to be interred in Dunwich Country.*'

He clapped his hands, and the sound was like an exclamation mark at the end of his sentence. Then he resumed. 'The undertaker, Hopkins, respected their wishes. I made him do that. He wanted to bury 'em, he wanted to bury 'em in the town graveyard out near Jacob's Pond, but I wouldn't let him. We had a terrible battle, believe me, young miss. But if I ever see Rice and Morgan again — I don't expect to, I don't think we get to go on once our flesh is finished, but I could be wrong, and if I am, and if I ever see Rice and Morgan again — I'm sure they'll thank me for making that fool Hopkins do what they wanted him to do.'

He stopped, short of breath after his long statement. But before Cordelia Whateley could speak, he put a question to her. 'How old do you think I am, young miss?'

She looked at him appraisingly. Her own great-grandfather, Cain Whateley, had lived to one hundred and nine, and

Armitage looked every bit as old as Cain had in his last days.

'I've read what I can find about the horror, and it says that you had a white beard in 1928. If you are the same Dr. Armitage . . . '

He gave her a sly grin. 'You've done your homework. I'd expect as much of an undecayed Whateley. I think I see a tinge of the Wizard himself in your face. Yes, I'm the same Henry Armitage. Shaved off my beard in '42. Hoped to get into the army then, and get out of Dunwich Country. *They* were onto me, though. Said I was too old, but I'd shaved it off by then so I kept it off.'

'But if you're the same Henry Armitage — ' Cordelia Whateley looked longingly at the chipped goblet of water but could not bring herself to take another sip. 'You were an old man in 1928, and that was nearly seventy years ago. That's impossible. You'd have to be — '

'Yes,' he nodded, 'I was almost eighty in 1928. I'm afraid I've given up on ever leaving Dunwich, but if the town is still here in a few years, I hope you'll come to my one hundred and fiftieth birthday party.'

He stood over her, reached down and patted her on the knee. Could this incredibly old man be — Cordelia Whateley shook her head. She must have misread the look in his eye. What she thought for a moment she had seen there was impossible.

She said, 'I don't mean to keep you up. I could come back in the morning. I mean,' she made a show of looking at the battery-powered watch on her wrist. She frowned and held it closer to the nearest oil-lamp. 'I just put a new battery in,' she muttered.

Armitage smiled. 'Electrical implements don't always work well in Dunwich. You did drive here, did you not, young miss?'

Cordelia Whateley nodded.

'You may have trouble starting your car in the morning.'

'But — '

'Never mind. We can dine at the inn. Then we can return here and I will assist you with your work as best I can. I have always felt a certain sense of — well, obligation is not exactly the word, but it will do — toward the Whateleys.'

Cordelia Whateley was flustered. 'You're very kind, Professor. But you need your sleep. A man your age — '

'I do not sleep,' Armitage replied. 'Come, let us go to the inn. We can walk from here.'

They walked from the Dunwich Institute back past Osborn's Store. The inn to which Armitage referred was not the restaurant Cordelia Whateley had seen, but another, located in a building that must have existed since the days of King George III and Governor Winthrop. They were waited on by a young woman — she could hardly have been into her teens, Cordelia Whateley realized — who seemed terrified of Henry Armitage. Armitage whispered a few words to the waitress, who nodded and disappeared into the kitchen, her long skirts brushing the floor behind her. Apparently Armitage had ordered for both of them, a custom that had gone out of fashion in Cordelia

Whateley's world long ago.

Cordelia Whateley looked around the room. Dour New Englanders of past centuries frowned down from framed canvases that lined the old wood-paneled walls. A small fire struggled fitfully to survive on a grey stone hearth. The only other illumination was furnished by oil-lamps. Beside the hearth a musician sat upon a high stool, picking out a tune on a stringed instrument that Cordelia Whateley did not recognize. The tune, however, seemed vaguely familiar: it was a transcription of a piano composition by the mad Russian composer Alexander Nikolayevich Scriabin.

The musician was a woman. At first glance she appeared to be aged, perhaps as much so as Henry Armitage himself, but as Cordelia Whateley studied the woman she realized that her hair was that of the albino rather than the crone. In her features, Cordelia Whateley suspected that she could detect a hint of the legendary Lavinia Whateley or — perhaps — of herself.

Without ceasing to play, the woman

raised her eyes from the fingerboard of her instrument and focused them upon Cordelia Whateley. Even in the faint light of wood flame and oil-lamp, it was clear that those eyes were hopelessly clouded by milk-white cataracts, cataracts the color of the woman's wild albino hair.

The only customers aside from Cordelia Whateley and Henry Armitage were a group of dark-clad persons wearing the uniform and insignia of the Dunwich Research Project.

After a few minutes one of them, a grey-haired, severe-visaged woman, approached their table. 'Professor Armitage,' she said sharply, 'I didn't know that you had invited a guest to visit you.'

Armitage said, 'I didn't invite her. She wrote and said she was coming from Canada. I couldn't prevent.'

I couldn't prevent, Cordelia mused. What an odd expression.

The uniformed woman nodded angrily and returned to her own table. Henry Armitage had not introduced Cordelia Whateley to her.

The waitress reappeared with a tray of

dishes and glasses. A dust-coated bottle stood on the tray as well. The waitress set the dishes and bottle on the table. Cordelia Whateley's dish held a slab of very rare meat — she assumed that it was beef. It was set off by a portion of broccoli and several very small roasted potatoes. Henry Armitage's dish was empty save for a sprig of parsley.

'Is that all you're going to eat?' Cordelia Whateley asked.

Armitage shook his head. 'I have had my nourishment.'

'But — I could have come here alone for dinner. You didn't need to — '

'It is not good to be alone on the streets of Dunwich after dark, young miss.' Armitage reached across the table and took Cordelia Whateley by the wrist. He held her briefly, then dropped his own hand to his lap. He wore a threadbare black suit, a white shirt with a frayed collar, and a bow tie in an abstract print that Cordelia Whateley found almost hypnotic in the flickering yellow light of the oil-lamp on their table.

'Why not? Is Dunwich unsafe? We have

muggers in Montreal, too, you know. I think I can protect myself.'

'Muggers?' A tiny laugh escaped Armitage's lips, but even so Cordelia Whateley noticed a reaction among the uniformed men and women at the other table. 'There are no muggers in Dunwich,' Armitage said. 'No, young miss. There are no muggers.'

After a long day's journey from her home in Montreal, Cordelia Whateley experienced a combination of hunger and fatigue. She lifted her knife and fork and prepared to slice the rare meat on her plate. Her usual preference was for meat more thoroughly roasted than this, but appetite and reluctance to provoke any disagreement in the inn caused her to plunge the tines of her fork into the roast, and then the sharp point of her knife.

Perhaps it was the dim and unsteady illumination in the inn coupled with the effects of fatigue and several sips of wine that created an illusion, but the meat appeared to *writhe* away from Cordelia Whateley's implements. An involuntary gasp escaped her. The uniformed diners and even the blind musician turned their eyes toward her. She whispered, 'Doctor Armitage, I'm — I'm afraid I've lost my appetite. If we could leave now, and we'll start our work in the morning . . . '

The ancient man shook his head negatingly. 'You must not put off. We will return to the Institute.'

Half fainting from fatigue and wine, yet equally eager to be at her work, Cordelia Whateley agreed. Upon returning to the Institute, Professor Armitage produced a ring of keys from the pocket of his shabby black suit and unlocked the glass-fronted bookcase containing the largest of the volumes Cordelia Whateley had previously seen.

He selected one and carried it to a heavy deal table beside which a wooden reading-chair had already been placed, and laid it carefully upon the table. 'You will find useful information here, young miss.' Having said this he retired to a far corner and folded himself into a chair. To Cordelia Whateley he seemed to disappear.

She examined the volume Armitage

had laid out. It was a bound collection of large news pages, the paper yellowing and flaking away at the edges.

'I thought everybody was transferring newspaper files to microfilm,' Cordelia Whateley said.

From his darkened corner, Henry Armitage replied, 'Many in Dunwich Town like things as they were.'

Cordelia Whateley, examining the masthead of the bound newspaper, read aloud, 'The Dunwich Daily Dispatch.'

'Only called it a daily,' Armitage commented. 'You could never tell when there'd be an issue. The editor, Ephraim Clay, used to say it was a daily, came out once a day, just not every day. I think that was some kind of joke. Never understood Ephraim very well. A strange man. But look at those issues for 1928. You'll learn all you need to know.'

Cordelia Whateley fumbled in her large purse and brought out a small tape recorder. She pressed a switch and began dictating segments from various 1928 issues of the *Dunwich Daily Dispatch*.

One of them, reprinted from a Boston

newspaper, reported the death of Cordelia's distant cousin, Wilbur Whateley. The article bore no byline, but it described the youthful, dying giant in shuddersome detail. Cordelia's voice quavered and shook as she spoke, but she managed to continue to the end of the article.

Above the waist it was semi-anthropomorphic (the dispatch ran) though its chest, where the dog's rending paws still rested watchfully, had the leathery, reticulated hide of a crocodile or alligator. The back was piebald with yellow and black, and dimly suggested the squamous covering of certain snakes. Below the waist, though, it was the worst; for here all human resemblance left off and sheer phantasy began. The skin was thickly covered with coarse black fur, and from the abdomen a score of long greenish-grey tentacles with red sucking mouths protruded limply. Their arrangement was odd, and seemed to follow the symmetries of some cosmic geometry unknown to earth or the solar system. On each of the hips, deep set in a kind of pinkish, ciliated orbit, was what seemed to be a rudimentary eye; whilst in lieu of a tail there depended a kind of trunk or feeler with purple annular markings, and with many evidences of being an undeveloped mouth or throat. The limbs, save for their black fur, roughly resembled the hind legs of prehistoric earth's giant saurians; and terminated in ridgy-veined pads that were neither hooves nor claws. When the thing breathed, its tail and tentacles rhythmically changed colour, as if from some circulatory cause normal to the non-human side of its ancestry. In the tentacles this was observable as a deepening of the greenish tinge, whilst in the tail it was manifest as a yellowish appearance which alternated with a sickly greyish-white in the spaces between the purple rings. Of genuine blood there was none; only the foetid greenish-yellow ichor which trickled along the painted floor beyond

26

the radius of the stickiness, and left a curious discolouration behind it.

Cordelia Whateley collapsed into the wooden reading-chair. She pressed her hands to her chest, trying to steady her breathing. After a while she managed to raise her face and peer into the darkened corner where Armitage sat, patiently waiting for her to speak.

Finally she managed to mumble, 'It's impossible. Impossible. I know my Cousin Wilbur was — not normal. Not like other men, even other Whateleys. But this — how could such a being exist?'

Armitage did not respond directly. Instead, he asked, 'Did you know that Wilbur was a twin?'

'No. My parents and grandparents would never speak of the Dunwich branch of the family. Only my great-grandfather, Cain Whateley, told me stories. I remember my parents were furious with him. I used to ask them about the Whateleys, but they would never tell me anything, and when I asked about things that Great-Grandfather Cain told me, they said it was all nonsense. They said he'd seen too many horror movies when he was a boy, and read too many cheap magazines, that he was so old he couldn't distinguish what he'd read about or seen in the movies from what was real.'

Armitage made a soft sound but spoke no words.

'Even Great-Grandfather Cain never mentioned Wilbur's being a twin.'

'But still he was,' Armitage told her. 'Read on.'

Cordelia Whateley felt a painful thirst; the wine she had sipped at the inn had left a dry aftertaste in her mouth and throat. But recollection of the malodoriferous water Armitage had offered her earlier militated against her renewing the request. Instead, she continued leafing through old *Dunwich Daily Dispatches*, pausing frequently to dictate excerpts into her miniature tape recorder.

A gasp of horror and revulsion escaped her when she came to the description of another creature, but she read the words aloud from the yellowing page, first attributing them accurately to still another cousin, Curtis Whateley. The reporter, once more anonymous, seemingly had seen fit to record Curtis Whateley's degenerate Miskatonic Valley speech in its full phonetic peculiarity:

Bigger'n a barn . . . all made o' squirmin' ropes . . . hull thing sort o' shaped like a hen's egg bigger'n anything with dozens o' legs like hogsheads that haff shut up when they step . . . nothin' solid abaout it — all like jelly, an' made o' sep 'rit wrigglin' ropes pushed close together . . . great bulgin' eyes all over it . . . ten or twenty maouths or trunks a-stickin' aout all along the sides, big as stove-pipes, an' all a-tossin' an' openin' an' shuttin' . . . all grey, with kinder blue or purple rings . . . an' Gawd in Heaven — that haff face on top!

And another quotation, from another news page, attributed to the same Curtis Whateley.

Oh, oh, my Gawd, that haff face
— that haff face on top of it . . . that
face with the red eyes an' crinkly albino
hair, an' no chin, like the Whateleys
. . . It was a octopus, centipede, spider
kind o' thing, but they was a
haff-shaped man's face on top of it, and
it looked like Wizard Whateley's, only
it was yards and yards acrost . . .

Cordelia Whateley collapsed, sobbing.
'That was Wilbur's brother.' Henry
Armitage spoke in an ancient, papery
voice. 'He never had a name, or if he did,
no one in all the Valley ever knew it. Save,
perhaps, Wilbur, or his mother, Lavinia.'
Armitage's breath rasped. 'Or mebbe his
step-father, old Wizard Whateley.'
Cordelia Whateley managed to raise
her eyes. She ran her fingers through her
hair. She had heard superstitious tales of
men or women whose hair had turned
white in a single night, from sheer terror.
She wondered if that was happening to
her. She wondered if she was going mad.
'What do you mean, step-father?' she
croaked. 'Wasn't Lavinia's husband the

real father? Who was, then?'

'Not old Wizard Whateley, you can be sartin.' Armitage was lapsing into the local argot.

'Who was the father?' Cordelia Whateley demanded.

Armitage uttered a frightening chuckle. He rose, an elongated, shadowy figure still obscured by darkness. To Cordelia Whateley he seemed unnaturally tall, perhaps as tall as her Cousin Wilbur's legendary stature. But maybe all was illusion, maybe all was the effect of the dim, flickering illumination of fireplace and oil-lamp.

'Wizard Whateley was not the father of the twins. Not any more than Joseph the Carpenter was the father of Jesus of Nazareth.' He paused. 'That is, ef you b'lieve that Christian balderdash, o' course. Ef you do, then the father was God, wa'nt he? An' Joseph merely the foster-father of the infant Jesus? Ef you believe that Christian balderdash, o' course.'

'Well, I — I've never thought about it very much, Professor.'

'Wilbur Whateley and his giant brother, his daemon brother, were star-spawn, young miss. Their father was a bein' from the vaults of space, a member of a civilization old beawond human comprehension an' distant beawond human imagination. An' he come here to earth — Gawd alone knows why — an' he fathered two sons awn the blessed Lavinia Whateley. An' the good people o' Dunwich Town kilt 'em. Yes, the good people o' Dunwich Town refused t' understand, refused t' care, refused t' give the slightest sympathy or assistance to them two innocent children of an alien father and an earthly mother. We kilt 'em. The Romans had nothin' on us. They kilt themselves one Son o' Gawd. We kilt us two. An' our punishment will be terrible, young miss. The stars are right, know it, young miss, the stars are right and our punishment will be terrible.'

A low moan escaped Cordelia Whateley. She had come to Professor Armitage in hopes of learning the truth about her cursed relatives, and instead had been subjected to the ravings of this madman.

'It's impossible,' she managed. 'An alien and a human could never inter-breed. It's a biological impossibility.'

'You think so?' Armitage challenged. He was growing calmer, and reverting from his Dunwich dialect into the cultured academic pronunciation he had used at first. 'A mere few years ago it might have seemed impossible, but we are learning better. Most of the people of Dunwich know little of such things, and such things have been wisely kept from them. But a few of us — those ones at the Project and I alone here at the Institute — we keep abreast of modern science. And we know that genetic material from one creature can be implanted within the ovum of another, even a creature of another species. Did you know that DNA extracted from a laboratory mouse and injected into the cells of a common fruit fly has produced eyes on the legs of that fly? Eyes, young miss, eyes! Think of what you've just read.'

'But — but it's horrid. It's blasphe-mous! How can you countenance such wickedness in the name of science?'

'Ah.' Armitage seemed pleased. He advanced toward Cordelia Whateley and stood with his back to the fireplace. His dark suit no longer seemed threadbare, his white hair appeared to stand out from his scalp like a hydra's snakes. He seemed to tower nearly to the high, echoing ceiling. He seemed simultaneously as young as an infant and as old as the continents. 'Ah,' he repeated, 'I suspect that you do believe in that religious nonsense. You use words like wickedness. Like blasphemy. Next you'll accuse us of sinning.'

'Yes,' she almost shouted. 'Yes. It is sinful!'

She thought she caught the flash of firelight glinting off Henry Armitage's teeth as he grinned down at her. 'He's coming, you know.'

'Nobody is coming.' She felt a growing desperation in the pit of her belly.

'But he is. He is. He's on his way now. You'll see.'

Cordelia Whateley pushed herself to her feet. 'I have to leave now.' She scrambled toward the door, clutching her purse in one hand and her small tape recorder in the other. 'Don't — don't help me — don't see me out — I'll find my own way.'

Armitage seemed to loom even taller. She couldn't understand how he managed to stay in the building without his head colliding with the rafters and beams overhead. But he did not pursue her. He merely stood with his back to the fireplace, hands balled in fists, resting on his hips.

And he laughed. He laughed, and he roared in a voice like the voice of a blaspheming godlet, 'The father is coming. He's coming to Sentinel Hill, young miss. And he's mad. You know what the students like to say? The few students we have left in this demon-damned town? He's coming back, young miss, and he's mad as hell!'

Cordelia Whateley plunged through the door and stood panting on the portico of the Dunwich Institute.

Behind her, through the open door, the voice of Henry Armitage boomed out, 'He'll come to Sentinel Hill. Trust me.

See if you can get in. He's coming to Sentinel Hill.'

Cordelia Whateley managed to fumble the keys to her conservative sedan from her oversized purse. She unlocked the automobile's door, plunged inside, started the engine after several tantalizing false attempts, switched on the lights and tore madly through the deserted Dunwich streets, heading finally for the outskirts of town and the installation at Sentinel Hill.

The grounds of the Dunwich Research Project were illuminated as glaringly as if it had been noontime on a brilliant day. Vaguely military-looking vehicles crowded the roads inside the gates and were parked helter-skelter around the buildings. The rolling gate itself had been left wide open and utterly untended, and Cordelia had no trouble driving her car onto the grounds and finding an opening near a cluster of military vehicles. They were parked halfway up Sentinel Hill, and Cordelia had to swing her sedan around the end of a row and leave it pointing downhill.

The giant radar dishes atop Sentinel Hill swung slowly in unison as if following a single object that approached from far overhead, invisible to the naked eye. Great searchlights like props from a monochromatic motion picture about a long-concluded war sped beams of vivid white light into the black night sky.

Men and women in the distinctive garb of the Dunwich Research Project raced past Cordelia Whateley, ignoring her utterly in their concentration on their assigned tasks.

Now a tiny speck appeared fleetingly in a searchlight beam. A woman near Cordelia Whateley pointed at it and shouted, 'He's coming, he's almost here!'

Cordelia Whateley watched until the black dot was picked up by another searchlight, and another. Near her a corpulent man in dark uniform fell to his knees on the oddly-colored New England grass. He held a book in his hands, and on its cover Cordelia Whateley recognized the illustration and the title as those she had seen in a locked bookcase at the Dunwich Institute.

Strangely, as the man knelt and opened the leather-bound volume, his costume seemed less to reflect a military origin than an ecclesiastical one. He began to read aloud, but in a language utterly unlike any that Cordelia Whateley had ever heard.

The speck in the sky was growing perceptibly larger. Cordelia Whateley had half-expected the Dunwich Research Project to be a branch of the American military establishment, most likely a refined version of the controversial Strategic Defense Initiative of former years. She half-expected to see missile-launchers rising from Sentinel Hill, and deadly rockets rising from them to destroy the thing that was growing larger with each passing moment.

But to her shock she realized that the open meadow beside Sentinel Hill was spread as a gigantic altar. It was covered with tapestries into which were woven depictions of blasphemous beings performing unspeakable acts upon writhing humans, their mouths open in silent screams of anguish and terror. And standing in the middle of the huge altar, naked, motionless, seemingly drugged, were men and women, boys and girls, clearly every missing person whose disappearance from the Miskatonic Valley and all of Dunwich Country for years past had gone unexplained.

And all around Cordelia Whateley dark-clad men and women were kneeling in adoration, singing and gesturing to that which drew closer and closer to them.

The thing was unbelievably huge. Cordelia Whateley revised her estimate of its size again and again, expecting it to land at any moment, but instead it grew, and it grew, filling the sky, blotting out the stars.

And in the illumination of the searchlights Cordelia Whateley could make out the shape of the thing. It was like a gargantuan jellyfish, literally miles in breadth. Thousands — no, millions — of tentacles dangled from its underside, writhing and squirming, stretching eagerly toward the hapless, naked victims who awaited them below.

The tentacles were greenish at their

base, and white along their expanse, and deep crimson at their tips. And as they approached the altar those tips opened to reveal rows of glittering, triangular teeth that snapped and gnashed in anticipation of their coming feast.

And among the tentacles, on thicker, longer stalks, were large, round, rolling eyeballs that flashed and shifted from victim to victim, from altar to sycophant. And around the edges of the being rows upon rows of ciliated, transluscent, gelatinous extensions rippled in repulsive rhythmic sequence.

Cordelia Whateley snapped to awareness as if awakening from a hypnotic trance. She raced across the meadow to her automobile and turned the key in the ignition. Nothing happened. But the car stood at the end of a row of vehicles halfway up Sentinel Hill, and she set the gear lever in neutral and released the parking brake, struggling with sheer will power to make the sedan roll downhill.

It did!

Just before the ground leveled out she shoved the gear lever into low, whispering a prayer. The engine caught and she sped through the open gate of the Dunwich Research Project. She kept the accelerator pressed to the floor, ignoring laws and obstacles equally, tears streaming down her cheeks and screams emerging from her mouth, until she reached the Aylesbury Pike.

Here she drew up and climbed from the car. She clambered onto its hood and from there onto its roof and turned her gaze back toward Dunwich. The distinctive shape of Sentinel Hill was silhouetted against distant clouds and stars.

The giant, jellyfish-thing was still settling. Cordelia Whateley realized now that even her greatest estimate of its size was grossly insufficient. It was larger than the altar, larger than Sentinel Hill, larger than the entire Dunwich Research Project compound.

It was easily as large as all of Dunwich Town.

And coming from it was a horrible, wet sound. A sucking, slithering, *hungry* sound. And from the ground beneath Dunwich, even as far away as the

Aylesbury Pike, could be felt a terrible, trembling, rumbling.

It could only have been a matter of minutes, perhaps even seconds, until the great creature struck the earth. All of the equipment on Sentinel Hill must have shorted in that moment, and for all that Cordelia Whateley was ever able to determine, it was the immense electrical field created by that equipment that caused all the other problems with electrical devices in Dunwich.

There was a flash brighter than the noonday sun, and a coruscation of pulsing colors, and a strange display of chromatics that Cordelia Whateley could only describe, in the days and years that followed, as *the very sky and earth screaming in terror and in pain*.

Then all was silence and all was darkness, and Cordelia Whateley knew nothing until she opened her eyes and looked into the face of a brawny individual wearing the garb of a Massachusetts State Trooper. He was shining a flashlight into her eyes, and when she blinked and moaned he said,

'Are you all right, ma'am?'

She lifted a hand to her face and said, 'Yes. Yes. I just — I managed to escape from Dunwich Town.'

The trooper frowned. 'There's been a terrible disaster there, ma'am. Looks as if some kind of giant meteor crashed on Dunwich. Wiped out the town, the whole entire town.' He shook his head. 'Every man, woman and child. And there's some kind of horrid goop all over the place, and a stench like to make you throw up. Pardon me, ma'am. Sorry about that.'

Cordelia Whateley struggled to stand up.

The trooper assisted her gently. 'Can we take you somewhere, ma'am? Is there someone we should notify?'

'No.' She shook her head. 'I just want to leave. I just want to get back to Montreal and forget this — this horror.'

The trooper's face was visible in the reflected illumination cast by his flashlight. 'Should a lady your age be driving a car?' he asked. 'Do you still have a driver's license, ma'am? I mean, I know the laws are different there in Quebec.

43

Your car has Quebec tags, ma'am. Are you from Quebec?'

She said, 'Yes. Thank you. I'm perfectly all right. I just want to get home.'

The trooper looked dubious, but finally he said, 'All right, ma'am. If you're sure you'll be all right.'

'I'm perfectly all right,' she repeated, annoyed. The trooper released her and she climbed into her car. Her purse lay on the seat beside her and she found the cassette player and rewound the tape and hit *play*. From the player's speaker there emerged only a hissing and crackling, and the occasional hint of an indecipherable whisper.

Cordelia shut the player off. She tossed it into the back seat of her automobile. She switched on the engine. This time it started without hesitation. She reached up to adjust the rear-view mirror, but on an impulse turned it first toward herself. By the dome-light of the sedan she studied her image. Her hair was white and her visage was the withered, wrinkled, desiccated face of a woman three times her age.

44

The Peltonville Horror

The Hudson-Terraplane roadster's electric headlights cut twin channels of brilliance through the swirling fog of the Peltonville Turnpike. The hour was late and traffic was almost nonexistent, save for the sporty little car's sleek, bright blue form.

The shrieking voice that had come from the automobile's custom-fitted Stromberg-Carlson radio gave way to the less disturbing and more polished tones of a staff announcer. 'Tune in again next week for another Witch's Tale,' he urged listeners. 'But for now, sit back and relax, put your feet up and enjoy the melodic musical stylings of the Stan Sawyer Orchestra.'

'What a relief!' Delia Davis managed a quiet little laugh, tinged with a suggestion of nervousness. 'I never did like those spooky programs, Paul, darling. If I didn't love you so much I don't think I could ever put up with them.'

'But, Delia,' Paul Carter reached across the seat to pat his sweetheart's hand, 'it's all just make-believe. You don't think there's really an old witch named Nancy who's more than a hundred years old, and lives with a wise black cat named Satan, do you?'

'No.' Delia hesitated. Then she repeated, 'No. I guess not.' Paul released her hand and she tightened the scarf over her head. Her hair was jet black; by candlelight Paul Carter said that it showed bits of midnight blue that matched the color of her eyes. Delia had let her hair grow longer now that the boyish look and the bobbed hair of the previous decade had been abandoned for a more feminine look. 'I do so love the feel of the wind and the smell of the fresh air out here in the country. But it's getting awfully cold now that the sun is down. Feels more like winter than spring.'

Paul laughed. 'Changing the subject, are you?'

'I guess so. When we crossed that

bridge over the Beeton River a while ago, I could just imagine we were flying through the stratosphere.' Delia reached for the tuning knob on the dashboard. The signal had drifted and she brought it back so the sound of saxophones and trumpets filled the convertible's tonneau. 'I guess I just don't enjoy being scared. Well, maybe just a little, like at those frightening movies. But then I know you'll put your arm around me and I feel all safe. I wish we were married, Paul. Then you could put your arm around me all the time and I'd never be frightened again. Oh, Paul, will we ever be married? Can't we even set a date?'

'As soon as this depression is over and the economy picks up again,' Paul replied. 'You know, I'm lucky to still have a job at all, but since they've been cutting salaries every few months, I can barely pay the rent on a furnished room. There's no way I could afford an apartment and support a wife.'

Delia lowered her eyes to the engagement ring on her left hand. 'We could sell my ring.' She toyed with the narrow band

and its tiny, glittering stone. 'And we don't really need a car. As much fun as it is, Paul, you could take the streetcar to work at the plant.'

Paul shook his head. 'I bought the car before the crash. Some timing, wasn't it? I couldn't get a quarter of what it's worth, now. And you'll never sell your ring, Delia, not as long as I can draw breath and do a day's work. Listen — '

Delia interrupted him with a gasp. 'Paul — what was that?'

'What, Delia? I didn't see anything.'

'Right over there, Paul. I thought I saw something moving in the woods, and then — then there was a flash. I don't know what it was. Something bright, a point of light, two points of light. No, there were more. They kept blinking on and off. I think there were eight of them. I — they were some color I've never seen before. Something like red, I think, but so deep, so powerful — so frightening . . . Oh, Paul, what could it be?'

Paul eased up on the roadster's accelerator and the little car slowed. 'I don't see anything, Delia. Through this fog, I don't know how you did. But maybe there was a momentary break. It might have been an electric power line or a radio tower. Or maybe you just caught sight of a couple of stars.'

'No, Paul. It was nothing like that. It was — oh, never mind. It's gone now, whatever it was. Let's go on.'

A distant flash lit the night sky above the woods to the west. Paul pushed the car to a higher speed. As he did so a low, distant rumble followed the lightning. 'Uh-oh. I hope we're not going to get rained on.'

'Maybe we should stop and put the top up.' Delia looked around them. The fog had largely lifted but the night had actually grown darker than ever. A bright moon struggled to send its light through thick storm clouds, but only an occasional break in the clouds permitted a brief moment of illumination.

Lightning flashed, closer and brighter, a sinister greenish sheet silhouetting dark, deciduous vegetation.

'Look!' Delia exclaimed, 'there it is again!' She pointed toward the east.

'Those lights, blinking like terrible, hungry eyes!'

This time Paul pulled the little car onto the shoulder of the road. He turned off the engine, followed Delia's pointing finger with his eyes. 'I don't see anything.'

'No,' Delia shook her head. 'They're gone. But wait, Paul, listen.' The radio had of course lapsed into silence when the roadster's ignition was cut, and the whisper of the gathering storm sounded through pines and oaks.

There was another flash of lightning. This time Paul counted the seconds until thunder boomed. 'What's the saying,' he muttered, 'a mile a second? That storm is only a few miles away now. In fact, I think I just felt the first raindrops on my face. Help me, Delia, let's get the top up!'

Delia cocked her head, 'Listen to that, dear.'

Paul frowned. 'I hear the wind and rain.'

'No, there's another sound. A sort of piping and hissing and scratching. Like some incredibly gigantic — oh, Paul, I don't know. Something horrible. Could there be a spider so huge that it towers above the trees? Is it possible?'

Paul put his arms around her. 'No, Delia. It's just the storm. The thunder and lightning and wind. Really, dear, it's just the storm.'

Paul fumbled for the three-cell flashlight that he kept in the Hudson-Terraplane. It blazed into light and he used it now as a work-lamp.

It took the effort of a few minutes to raise the canvas top on the little roadster and button it in place. Even so, Paul and Delia were halfway to a good drenching by the time they scrambled back into the car and slammed the side doors that turned it into a snug refuge from the storm. With the optimism of youth they laughed off their wet condition. Delia undid her scarf and primped her raven curls with a brush she'd carried in her purse.

Paul ran his fingers through his own rust-colored hair. He was overdue for a trim; the hair was beginning to curl over his collar. He turned the ignition key and mashed down on the self-starter switch with his heavy brogan. The Hudson-Terraplane's six-cylinder engine coughed once as if clearing its throat of the falling rain, then purred happily. Paul switched on the headlights. The fog had disappeared now, and twin shafts of raindrops appeared before the roadster.

'What shall it be, darling?' he asked. 'Shall we push on or turn back to Springfield?'

Delia hummed for a moment, a habit of hers while considering choices. 'I could do with a cup of warm soup beside a friendly fireplace, dear. Isn't there a roadhouse somewhere along the Peltonville Pike?'

Paul's brow furrowed in thought. 'I'm pretty sure there is. I've only been to Peltonville a few times, but I think I recall seeing one not far beyond the Beeton River bridge.'

'Oh, let's push on then, Paul. It's such a miserable night, the ride home wouldn't be any fun at all with our clothes all clammy and cold as they are.'

'No sooner said than done!' He pulled the car back onto the blacktop highway.

'It's a good thing they paved over the old dirt road, isn't it!'

The roadster's tires hissed over the rain-swept blacktop. Now a few unseasonable hailstones were mixed with the drops. They clattered and bounced off the Hudson-Terraplane's hood and began to accumulate on the road surface as well. Winds pushed the lightweight car sideways but Paul Carter's skillful hands kept the roadster on a steady course. He reached to switch on the Stromberg-Carlson, but the lightning's interference and the noise of the storm, which had now struck in its full fury, made it impossible to hear anything worthwhile. Paul switched the radio back off.

He felt Delia's head resting on his shoulder and patted her hand with his own. Soon a sign appeared beside the highway, advertising Daniello's Roadhouse two miles ahead. Paul pushed on. Shortly there was another sign. *Daniello's*, it read, *Steaks, Cocktails, Dancing to Willie Moore's African Chili Seven.*

Daniello's Roadhouse was a pleasant-looking establishment built in the popular

Tudor Revival style, with cream-colored stucco walls marked by half-timbered beams. At least, that was the way it appeared in the spotlights placed to illuminate its exterior. There was a neon sign on the roof, and the windows of stained diamond-glass showed an inviting amber color.

'We're here, Delia.' Paul placed a gentle kiss on his sweetheart's forehead.

Delia smiled up at him sleepily, then leaned away and stretched like a contented kitten.

The roadhouse door was made of heavy wooden planks and swung heavily on old iron hinges. Stepping inside, they were enveloped by the pleasant odors of hot, hearty cooking. They made their way to a lounge and found space for themselves on dark leather barstools. They could hear the sound of music coming from another room. Willie Moore's African Chili Seven lived up to their name. A hot version of 'Decatur Street Stomp' drifted into the lounge.

A red-jacketed bartender asked for their order. Paul ordered a hot toddy.

Delia giggled and asked for a tequila sunset. The lounge was not crowded. A few couples sat at tables. The other barstools were mostly unoccupied. The bartender placed their drinks in front of Paul and Delia and remarked that they were fortunate to make it safely through the storm.

'Why is that?' Paul asked.

The bartender pointed over his shoulder. On the shelf behind him stood a cathedral-topped Capehart radio. 'Can't get anything now, but earlier the news said that the bridge was out. Beeton River's rising and the bridge couldn't stand the gaff.'

Paul and Delia lifted their glasses in a silent toast. Paul introduced himself and Delia to the bartender.

'Mustafa Cristopolous,' the bartender identified himself. Now Paul realized that his speech was unusual, more an oddity of intonation than an actual accent. His voice was deep and sounded like a truckload of gravel. 'I am half Greek, half Turkish,' the bartender explained. 'I was born in Izmir. I don't suppose you've ever heard of that place.' His face carried the marks of past experiences. His nose had been broken more than once, an oddly appealing dimple marked the center of his chin and an old scar on one cheek had faded now but looked as if it had once been livid. The absence of hair on his skull was made up for by a huge black moustache.

'In the old country the Greeks hated me because I was Turkish and the Turks hated me because I was Greek. So I come to America. Here, everybody's everything.'

'But what about the bridge?' Delia asked.

'Big storm,' Cristopolous growled. 'The boss don't like me playing the radio when the band is on, but I like to listen to news. I get stations from Springfield, Aurora, Littleton. News on the Springfield station says too much debris coming down the Beeton River, jammed up under the bridge, roadway cracked. They won't even have crews there till after the storm is over.'

He looked toward the entrance of the

roadhouse as if he could see outside. 'How bad is it now?'

Paul said, 'It got pretty nasty, Mustafa. Rain turning to hail.'

The big bartender nodded his understanding. Paul had finished his drink now, and Delia's glass was mostly empty. Cristopolous asked if they wanted a refill but instead they left the lounge and moved to the dining room. The African Chili Seven were playing 'Deep Bayou Blues.' Paul and Delia found a table and a waitress took their order. Paul asked for a sirloin steak. Delia asked for chicken. Both requested soup before their entrées.

While they ate they discussed what to do next. Clearly there was no point in trying to return to Springfield. They would get as far as the bridge and have to wait for repairs to be made.

'I'm afraid we'll have to continue on to Peltonville,' Paul announced.

'But then we won't get back to Springfield until tomorrow at the soonest,' Delia complained. 'What will people think? Mother and Dad will be beside themselves. And all our friends, Paul

— do you think it's right?'

He reached across the table and took her hand. 'I'm afraid we don't have much choice. Besides, people will just have to think what they choose.'

'I don't know.' Delia frowned. 'It's not as if we were married.' Then, 'Do you think there's an inn at Peltonville? If we got two rooms it might be all right. And if there's a telephone, I could call Mother and Dad and explain what happened.'

'A good idea, darling, but in a storm like this one, if the bridge is out, you can be sure that the telephone lines are down, too. I'm sorry. But if your parents really love you and trust you, they'll stand by you. As for anyone else — well, we'll just have to see it through.'

As they were leaving the roadhouse they stopped to speak with Mustafa Cristopolous once again. Paul asked how much farther it would be to Peltonville, and whether Mustafa thought the road would be drivable now. The bartender said it was only another dozen miles, and the road was a good one.

'I'm worried about the hail, though,' Paul explained.

Cristopolous shrugged his massive shoulders. 'Life is risky.' He paused, then added, 'But you be careful. Some bad things happen in Peltonville.'

'What bad things?'

'Just bad things. There is an old synagogue there, people do not go any more. Good people, I mean. Good people have mostly left Peltonville. You be careful, Paul and Delia.'

Cristopolous had remembered their names. Paul found small comfort in that. He asked, 'What do you mean by that — about the synagogue, I mean.'

A weary smile creased the bartender's battered features. He leaned across the polished mahogany and lowered his voice. 'Did I tell you, I am myself a Jew?' He looked around as if worried that he might be overheard. 'One more reason I left Europe. Bad enough to be both a Turk and a Greek. Being a Jew as well — that was enough to make everybody hate me. Here in America — well, no place is perfect, is it?' He nodded toward the

African Chili Seven. 'They still have to struggle. But if they were in Greece or in Turkey, they would have it far worse.'

Paul was still concerned about the Peltonville synagogue. He pressed Cristopolous for information. Cristopolous told him that he had once been a member of the congregation. It was called Temple Beth Shalom — the House of Peace. But the old rabbi had been forced to leave and a new leader took control. The old rabbi, Yacoub ben Yitzak, Jacob son of Isaac, replaced by Yeshua ben Yeshua, Joshua son of Joshua.

Ben Yeshua was a kabalist. He introduced ancient Hebrew magic into the synagogue. Its name had been changed to Temple Beth Mogen, House of the Star. The old congregants had all left Peltonville, those who had not mysteriously disappeared before they could get away. Cristopolous was one of the lucky ones, he had avoided Peltonville ever since. Other Jews had come from far away to replace them and fill the ranks of Temple Beth Mogen.

'It's very bad, Paul. If you go to

Peltonville, be very careful.'

Once they were back in the car and Paul had the engine warming up, Delia turned toward him, the reflected light of the sign on Daniello's Roadhouse showing her worried expression. 'Do you think we can make it to Peltonville, Paul?'

'There are other patrons. They didn't look too worried to me.'

'But there's something else.'

Paul turned and took her in his arms, comforting her. 'What, sweetheart? Are you still worried about your reputation? I promise, I'll stand by you whatever they say.'

'No, it isn't that, Paul. It's — remember those lights, those eyes, I thought they were. And that weird sound. They were real, you know. I could tell you didn't believe me, I know you too well to be fooled. There was something there.'

'Oh, yes. A giant spider, was it?'

'I don't know. Maybe it was. Maybe something else. But there was something there, something alive. Oh, I don't like it. I don't know what it is, but I know it isn't nice at all.'

Paul leaned back and looked into Delia's eyes. 'If there was a monster loose in these woods, don't you think we'd have heard about it? Wouldn't there be stories in the Springfield *Courier* or reports on the radio? That's just the kind of thing they love to report. It's a nice change from weddings and Rotary Club meetings and high school basketball games. You haven't read anything about a monster, have you?'

'No,' she admitted. 'But still — I saw those lights and I heard that sound. You don't have to believe me but I know it was real, Paul, I know it!'

'Really, Delia — on a night like this, you were halfway asleep, we'd been listening to that spooky radio program, your imagination was playing tricks on you.'

'But what about that evil rabbi? That whole story about the Jewish synagogue in Peltonville. I've been in a synagogue in Springfield. My friend Rebecca was married in a synagogue, I was in the wedding. It was a beautiful service. I don't see how it could be evil, any more than a regular church could be evil, but Mr. Cristopolous didn't seem to be making that up.'

Paul shook his head. 'Old world superstitions, Delia. Just look at the man. He's had a hard life. Heaven knows what terrible experiences he must have had in Europe. He was lucky to get out of there and come to America, from the things that are going on now. I don't think he was making it up either, but his head is so full of wild folktales, he could believe anything.'

He turned on the headlights and backed the Hudson-Terraplane away from the roadhouse. In moments the little car was back on the highway. The storm had passed, the moon was bright and a black sky was dotted with colorful, distant stars that glittered like ice crystals in candlelight. The combination of moonlight, starlight and the roadster's headlamps showed the surface of the roadway, now white with crusted hail-stones.

Paul reached to switch on the little car's radio. He twirled the tuning knob.

On the Springfield and Aurora frequencies there was only hissing and crackling, but he managed to pick up a signal from Peltonville. He shook his head. 'Is that music? Chanting? I can't understand a word of it. And it all sounds so weird.'

Delia said, 'I think it's Hebrew. The service at Rebecca's wedding was partly in Hebrew. I don't know what it means, of course, but that sounds like the service.'

Paul tried to get a stronger signal but the best he could do was a faint chanting in an exotic tongue. He reached to turn off the radio but before he could do so the chanting faded into the background. Over it there came a hissing, piping, scraping noise, followed by the sound of voices exclaiming in ecstasy.

Even though the storm had passed, there was another flash of greenish lightning that seemed to come from all directions at once. The Hudson-Terraplane's engine sputtered into silence that was broken by an ear-shattering boom of thunder. Paul and Delia clutched each other's hands in alarm, then Paul managed a nervous chuckle. He grasped the steering wheel of the roadster and mashed down on the self-starter switch.

The little car's engine coughed once, then roared back to life. The orange light behind the radio's tuning dial glowed but there was no sound so Paul switched it off. He threw in the clutch, put the roadster in gear and set it to moving.

When they passed the Peltonville city limit Paul read the welcoming sign and population figures. Based on his recollection of his last visit he'd thought that Peltonville was bigger than the number indicated. Perhaps the latest census figures had shown a loss of population. Then he thought of Mustafa Cristopolous's words about Peltonville: *Good people have mostly left Peltonville. You be careful, Paul and Delia.*

It was hard for Paul or Delia to tell much about the character of Peltonville as the little roadster rolled into the downtown area. Every building seemed to be dark. Small houses in the style of the previous century loomed to left and right, but apparently Peltonvilliers retired early, for only the jagged silhouettes of the residences could be seen outlined against the backdrop of the night sky.

'Can you tell what time it is?' Paul asked.

Delia found the flashlight they had used earlier and shone its beam against her Elgin wristwatch. 'It's 10:30,' she announced. 'I guess they keep going at Daniello's Roadhouse but people in Peltonville don't stay up.'

After a few blocks lined by small retail shops the Hudson-Terraplane's head-lamps picked out a building with a darkened marquee extending over the crumbling sidewalk. Paul pulled the car to the curb and Delia shone the flashlight on the sign.

Peltonville Inn, it read.

'Well, that's straightforward enough,' Paul commented. 'Let's see if they can put us up for the night.'

'Paul.' Delia took his arm.

He looked at her, waiting to hear what she had to say.

'Paul, you know I love you, dear. You

do know that, don't you?'

'Of course, Delia. You shouldn't even have to ask. But — what's the matter?'

'Well — ' She looked down. 'Well, I'd really love to stay with you tonight. It would be — thrilling, Paul. But I know it would be wrong. I don't want to disappoint you, but would you mind if — if we took two rooms, dear?'

Paul shook his head. 'Of course not. What sort of fellow do you think I am?'

He climbed out of the Hudson-Terraplane, walked around the car and opened Delia's door. 'Come, darling, let's see what the management has to say to two poor travelers with no luggage to show for themselves!'

As Paul helped Delia from the car he realized that her breath was freezing in the air, as was his own. The wind had reversed its direction and brought the unseasonable storm back over Peltonville, or perhaps this was merely another front in a series. In any case, the wind had begun to howl unpleasantly and hail was battering both travelers.

Paul and Delia hustled to a place of

shelter beneath the marquee of the Peltonville Inn. The hotel was dark. Turning back toward the street they observed that the town had not yet converted its street lamps to electric power from the older gas illumination. A few fixtures flickered feebly despite the icy wind that swept the street.

Paul searched his trousers for a coin. He found a silver dollar and used it to rap on the glass panel of the Peltonville Inn's main entrance, but to no avail. He called out but his voice disappeared into the whistling, howling gale.

Stepping to the edge of the sheltered space beneath the marquee he held Delia to him, gazing at the sky. Clouds like shreds of torn black cloth swept overhead; in the breaks between them stars glared down at the couple. Never had Paul seen them so cold and seemingly malevolent. To the east a new constellation appeared, a group of eight stars of a color he had never seen before. If he had needed to name their color he would have called it red, but it was red of a shade and quality he had never previously experienced. The stars danced. Paul shuddered. An eerie auditory amalgam, part whistle, part hiss, part scraping, sounded faintly.

'There's nobody here,' he muttered. 'I can't tell, Delia, either the inn is out of business or it's closed for the night. Either way, we'll find no shelter here tonight.'

'But Paul,' she replied. Paul looked into her face. Clearly she was struggling to summon her courage but there were tears in her eyes and the corners of her mouth quivered. 'What will we do? Is there any place we can go? We can't just sleep in the car, we'll freeze.'

She was right, he realized. The wind whipped through their lightweight garments. Even beneath the marquee of the Peltonville Inn the hailstones bounced from the sidewalk and roadway and stung them like wave after wave of angry ice-hornets.

Across the street a faint light flickered in the windows of an old, two-story building. There was a momentary break in the screaming wind and a low chanting, barely audible, drifted to their ears. Paul stepped out from beneath the marquee, shielding his eyes from the pelting of hailstones as sharp and vicious as a bombardment of granite needles.

Yes, there was a light in the building.

Paul raised his gaze. The sinister constellation had disappeared from its previous location. Now it appeared once again, swooping and gyrating above the lighted building.

'There's somebody over there,' Paul exclaimed. 'Come on, Delia, they'll have to let us in!'

Hand in hand they ran from the Peltonville Inn to the lighted building across the street. The building loomed above them. The light they had seen flickered through a circular stained glass window. Its pattern was regular in shape, oddly suggestive of a sheriff's badge. Paul found himself wondering crazily if there wasn't a sheriff's station or town police headquarters here in Peltonville, if he and Delia should not have tried to find the authorities and pleaded with them for assistance against the cold and desolation of the darkness and the storm.

But it was too late for that.

Paul pounded on the heavy wooden door and found, to his surprise, that it swung open beneath his blows. He urged Delia in ahead of himself, then stepped into the shelter of the building, drawing the door shut behind them.

Clearly they were in a house of worship. The stained glass window behind them centered around a huge star formed of interlocking equilateral triangles. Paul had seen the pattern before, but there was something wrong with it this time. Each of the star's six points was surmounted by another figure, a clutching claw, a hook, or some other disquieting image. And in the center of the hexagon formed by the major triangles he saw a face such as his most horrifying nightmare had never brought to him, a face whose inhuman features were exceeded in their fearsomeness only by the malevolence of their expression, a face surrounded by dripping tentacles that appeared for all the world to writhe and clutch even as he watched.

Hand in hand Paul and Delia advanced into the sanctuary. The chamber was illuminated by a series of gas mantles mounted on pilasters. There appeared now the massed congregants, robed figures of indeterminate gender. Human they seemed, but somehow and in some incomprehensible way, *wrong*. They stood in a circle, swaying rhythmically and chanting.

In the center of the circle towered a massive figure, broad-shouldered, bearded, wearing a skull-cap and fringed shawl embroidered with kabalistic symbols and horrifying images. The figure raised his voice and his arms, but where Paul expected to see hands emerging from the sleeves of his robe were frightening claws that clacked angrily, wreathed by tentacles that wove and snapped like miniature whips.

The robed chanters surrounding their foul leader parted ranks. More quickly than Paul could follow they formed themselves into two rows. Those closest to Paul and Delia reached and took them by the hands. Paul's will was frozen. He stumbled forward, Delia at his side, passed from couple to couple of the frightening chanters, until they found themselves standing in the center of the newly reconstituted circle.

The leader loomed over them, far taller and more massive than any human being had the right to be. His arms were still raised, the claws and tentacles still performing their terrible gyrations. Involuntarily Paul raised his eyes, following the direction of the massive arms. Out of the corner of his vision he saw that Delia had done the same, and that even the monstrous figure before them had thrown back its head and was gazing in a state of spiritual rapture into the sky.

Yes, the sky loomed overhead. A retractable panel had been drawn back in the roof of the sanctuary. The hail had ceased to fall, but an icy wind howled through the aperture. The sound of the chanting rose, the leader began a strange and frightening dance, and in the blackness above the building, against the backdrop of faint, distant stars, the foul eight-pointed constellation appeared once more.

Only now Paul realized that the points of illumination were not distant stars but the eyes of a dreadful being, a being something like a huge spider, something like a frightening marine creature, something unholy and infinitely evil.

The eight red eyes drew nearer and the other features of the being became visible, fangs that dripped venom that steamed and sputtered as it struck the sanctuary floor, rope-like excrescencies that writhed and reached for the figures gathered beneath.

The chanting that surrounded Paul and Delia rose in pitch and urgency, the looming clergyman who stood before them lowered his arms and reached for Paul and Delia, seizing one of them in each arm, drawing them to his body that seemed to be more a chitinous shell than mere muscle and bone.

With immense and effortless strength he raised them, Paul in one horrid tentacle-circled claw, Delia in the other. Overhead the monstrous entity nodded and hissed, lowering itself toward the sacrifice that was clearly intended for it.

Paul reached for Delia, hoping in what must surely be the last moments of their lives to clasp her hand, but instead there was a monstrous crash and an icy blast as the massive doors of the building burst open and smashed to the floor. Paul was able to twist in the clergyman's grasp.

Standing in the doorway of the sanctuary was a figure he recognized at once as belonging to Mustafa Cristopolous, the Greek-Turkish-Jewish bartender whom Paul and Delia had met earlier in the evening at Daniello's Roadhouse.

But now Cristopolous was transformed. No longer bent over a mahogany surface, no longer clad in a brass-buttoned, red service jacket, Cristopolous seemed to have grown to a height half-again his previous size. His shoulders bulged with muscles. His features, the broken nose, the cleft chin, had assumed a nobility that Paul had not recognized in them in Daniello's cocktail lounge. The jagged scar on his cheek was no longer a pallid reminder of a long-ago wound, but a blazing talisman of righteous rage.

The low, accented voice that Paul and Delia had heard at Daniello's now roared its challenge in words of ancient Hebrew.

Among them Paul recognized a phrase that he had previously heard, *Yeshua ben Yeshua*. The evil clergyman, startled, dropped Paul and Delia. The entity that writhed above the sanctuary hissed and writhed in rage, deprived, at least for the moment, of its sacrificial prey.

The chanting congregants parted in terror, scurrying to cower among the pews and against the walls of the sanctuary.

Cristopolous strode forward, passing between Paul and Delia as he approached the clergyman. Cristopolous reached for the other, his massive hands clutching for the other's throat. The two were of a size and well matched in strength. They bellowed imprecations at each other, both of them growling in the same archaic tongue that Cristopolous had used to issue his first challenge upon entering the sanctuary. But among the alien words of Yeshua ben Yeshua, Paul was sure that he heard the name Yacoub ben Yitzak.

The clergyman and Cristopolous clutched each other in a dreadful parody of a lovers' embrace. The clergyman was clawing at Cristopolous's face and throat; Cristopolous held the other by his waist, lifting him from the floor by main strength.

From above the writhing, seething tangle, a foul cluster of tentacles descended, dripping venom and slime. Ropelike organs wrapped themselves around the two struggling figures, then raised both, slowly, from the floor. Paul reached for Cristopolous's heavy ankles. For a moment he secured a grip on them and felt himself actually lifted from his own feet, but a burning blob of slime spattered on one of his hands. In agony he lost his grasp on Cristopolous's ankle with that hand; the other, alone, had not sufficient strength to maintain its grip.

Paul collapsed back onto the floor. Delia knelt beside him, her arms around him, her tear-stained face pressed against his. Above them Paul saw Cristopolous and the clergyman, now wholly enveloped in a cocoon of writhing, ropelike tentacles, disappear into the gaping maw of the hideous entity that hovered briefly above the sanctuary, then rose with incredible speed until it disappeared once and for all into the starry sky above.

Again a cold wind swept into the sanctuary, and again the clatter of hailstones filled the night, this time pouring unimpeded through the open roof into the ancient building.

Taking Delia by the hand, Paul made his way from the building. The misshapen congregants whose chanting had earlier filled the building and the night had disappeared. Hand-in-hand, Paul and Delia made their way back to the Hudson-Terraplane.

Together, Paul and Delia turned back for one last sight of the desecrated synagogue. The monstrous creature was nowhere to be seen; it had disappeared along with both Yeshua ben Yeshua and Yacoub ben Yitzak. But from the swirling clouds overhead a single lurid shaft of shockingly ruddy lightning crackled downward. It must have struck the gas line that fed the mantles in the synagogue. There was a deafening explosion and the building disappeared, fragments clattering down for city blocks in all directions.

'We can't stay in Peltonville,' Paul announced. This assertion drew no objection from Delia. 'And we can't get back to Springfield until the bridge is repaired. But we can press on. Aurora isn't too much farther, and we can find accommodations there.' He paused. Then he added, 'Even if we can only find one room.'

Delia leaned her head against his shoulder and wrapped her arms around him. 'One room is all we'll need, Paul,' she murmured.

The Devil's Hop Yard

It was in the autumn of 1928 that those terrible events which came to be known as the Dunwich Horror transpired. The residents of the upper Miskatonic Valley in Massachusetts, at all times a taciturn breed of country folk never known for their hospitality or communicativeness toward outsiders, became thereafter positively hostile to such few travelers as happened to trespass upon their hilly and infertile region.

The people of the Dunwich region in particular, a sparse and inbred race with few intellectual or material attainments to show for their generations of toil, gradually became fewer than ever in number. It was the custom of the region to marry late and to have few children. Those infants delivered by the few physicians and midwives who practiced thereabouts were often deformed in some subtle and undefinable way; it would be impossible for an observer to place his finger upon the exact nature of the defect, yet it was plain that something was frighteningly wrong with many of the boys and girls born in the Miskatonic Valley.

Yet, as the years turned slowly, the pale, faded folk of Dunwich continued to raise their thin crops, to tend their dull-eyed and stringy cattle, and to wring their hard existence from the poor, farmed-out earth of their homesteads.

Events of interest were few and petty; the columns of the Aylesbury *Transcript*, the Arkham *Advertiser*, and even the imposing Boston *Globe* were scanned for items of diversion. Dunwich itself supported no regular newspaper, not even the slim weekly sheet that subsists in many such semi-rural communities.

It was therefore a source of much local gossip and a delight to the scandalmongers when Earl Sawyer abandoned Mamie Bishop, his common-law wife of twenty years standing, and took up instead with Zenia Whateley. Sawyer was an uncouth dirt farmer, some fifty years of age. His cheeks covered perpetually with a stubble that gave him the appearance of not having shaved for a week, his nose and eyes marked with the red lines of broken minor blood vessels, and his stoop-shouldered, shuffling gait marked him as a typical denizen of Dunwich's hilly environs.

Zenia Whateley was a thin, pallid creature, the daughter of old Zebulon Whateley and a wife so retiring in her lifetime and so thoroughly forgotten since her death that none could recall the details of her countenance or even her given name. The latter had been painted carelessly on the oblong wooden marker that indicated the place of her burial, but the cold rains and watery sunlight of the round of Dunwich's seasons had obliterated even this trace of the dead woman's individuality.

Zenia must have taken after her mother, for her own appearance was unprepossessing, her manner cringing, and her speech so infrequent and so diffident that few could recall ever having heard her voice. The loafers and gossips at Osborn's General Store in Dunwich were hard put to understand Earl Sawyer's motives in abandoning Mamie Bishop for Zenia Whateley. Not that Mamie was noted for her great beauty or scintillating personality; on the contrary: she was known as a meddler and a snoop, and her sharp tongue had stung many a denizen hoping to see some misdemeanor pass unnoted. Still, Mamie had within her that spark of vitality so seldom found in the folk of the upper Miskatonic, that trait of personality known in the rural argot as gumption, so that it was puzzling to see her perched beside Earl on the front seat of his rattling Model T Ford, her few belongings tied in slovenly bundles behind her, as Sawyer drove her over the dust-blowing turnpike to Aylesbury where she took quarters in the town's sole, dilapidated rooming house.

The year was 1938 when Earl Sawyer and Mamie Bishop parted ways. It had been a decade since the death of the poor, malformed giant Wilbur Whateley and the dissolution — for this word, rather than *death*, best characterizes the end of that monster — of his even more gigantic and even more shockingly made twin brother. But now it was the end of May, and the spring thaw had come late and grudgingly to the hard-pressed farmlands of the Miskatonic Valley this year.

When Earl Sawyer returned, alone, to Dunwich, he stopped in the center of the town, such as it was, parking his Model T opposite Osborn's. He crossed the dirty thoroughfare and climbed onto the porch of old Zebulon Whateley's house, pounding once upon the grey, peeling door while the loafers at Osborn's stared and commented behind his back.

The door opened and Earl Sawyer disappeared inside for a minute. The loafers puzzled over what business Earl might have with Zebulon Whateley, and their curiosity was rewarded shortly when Sawyer reappeared leading Zenia Whateley by one flaccid hand. Zenia wore a thin cotton dress, and through its threadbare covering it was obvious even from the distance of Osborn's that she was with child.

Earl Sawyer drove home to his dusty

farm, bringing Zenia with him, and proceeded to install her in place of Mamie Bishop. There was little noticeable change in the routine at Sawyer's farm with the change in its female occupant. Each morning Earl and Zenia would rise, Zenia would prepare and serve a meagre repast for them, and they would breakfast in grim silence. Earl would thereafter leave the house, carefully locking the door behind him with Zenia left inside to tend to the chores of housekeeping, and Earl would spend the entire day working out-of-doors.

The Sawyer farm contained just enough arable land to raise a meager crop of foodstuffs and to support a thin herd of the poor cattle common to the Miskatonic region. The bleak hillside known as the Devil's Hop Yard was also located on Sawyer's holdings. Here had grown no tree, shrub or blade of grass for as far back as the oldest archives of Dunwich recorded, and despite Earl Sawyer's repeated attempts to raise a crop on its unpleasant slopes, the Hop Yard resisted and remained barren. Even so there persisted reports of vague, unpleasant rumblings and cracklings from beneath the Hop Yard, and occasionally shocking odors were carried from it to adjoining farms when the wind was right.

On the first Sunday of June, 1938, Earl Sawyer and Zenia Whateley were seen to leave the farmhouse and climb into Sawyer's Model T. They drove together into Dunwich village, and, leaving the Model T in front of old Zebulon Whateley's drab house, walked across the churchyard, pausing to read such grave markers as remained there standing and legible, then entered the Dunwich Congregational Church that had been founded by the Reverend Abijah Hoadley in 1747. The pulpit of the Dunwich Congregational Church had been vacant since the unexplained disappearance of the Reverend Isaiah Ashton in the summer of 1912, but a circuit-riding Congregational minister from the city of Arkham conducted services in Dunwich from time to time.

This was the first occasion of Earl

Sawyer's attendance at services within memory, and there was a nodding of heads and a hissing of whispers up and down the pews as Earl and Zenia entered the frame building. Earl and Zenia took a pew to themselves at the rear of the congregation and when the order of service had reached its conclusion they remained behind to speak with the minister. No witness was present, of course, to overhear the conversation that took place, but later the minister volunteered his recollection of Sawyer's request and his own responses.

Sawyer, the minister reported, had asked him to perform a marriage. The couple to be united were himself (Sawyer) and Zenia Whateley. The minister had at first agreed, especially in view of Zenia's obvious condition, and the desirability of providing for a legitimate birth for her expected child. But Sawyer had refused to permit the minister to perform the usual marriage ceremony of the Congregational Church, insisting instead upon a ceremony involving certain foreign terms to be provided from some ancient documents handed down through the family of the bride.

Nor would Sawyer permit the minister to read the original documents, providing in their place crudely rendered transcripts written by a clumsy hand on tattered, filthy scraps of paper. Unfortunately the minister no longer had even these scraps. They had been retained by Sawyer, and the minister could recall only vaguely a few words of the strange and almost unpronounceable incantations he had been requested to utter: *N'gai, n'gha'ghaa, bugg-shoggog,* he remembered. And a reference to a lost city 'between the Yr and the Nhhngr.'

The minister had refused to perform the blasphemous ceremony requested by Sawyer, holding that it would be ecclesiastically improper and possibly even heretical of him to do so, but he renewed his offer to perform an orthodox Congregational marriage, and possibly to include certain additional materials provided by the couple *if he were shown a translation also,* so as to convince himself of the propriety of the ceremony.

Earl Sawyer refused vehemently, warning the minister that he stood in far greater peril should he ever learn the meaning of the words than if he remained in ignorance of them. At length Sawyer stalked angrily from the church, pulling the passive Zenia Whateley behind him, and returned with her to his farm.

A few nights later the couple were visited by Zenia's father, old Zebulon Whateley, and also by Squire Sawyer Whateley, of the semi-undecayed Whateleys, a man who held the unusual distinction of claiming cousinship to both Earl Sawyer and Zenia Whateley. At midnight the four figures, Earl, Zenia, old Zebulon, and Squire Whateley, climbed slowly to the top of the Devil's Hop Yard. What acts they performed at the crest of the hill are not known with certainty, but Luther Brown, now a fully-grown man and engaged to be married to George Corey's daughter Olivia, stated later that he had been searching for a lost heifer near the boundary between Corey's farm and Sawyer's, and saw the four figures silhouetted against the night constellations as they stood atop the hill.

As Luther Brown watched, all four disrobed; he was fairly certain of the identification of the three men, and completely sure of that of Zenia because of her obvious pregnancy. Completely naked they set fire to an altar of wood apparently set up in advance on the peak of the Hop Yard. What rites they performed before Luther fled in terror and disgust he refused to divulge, but later that night loud cracking sounds were heard coming from the vicinity of the Sawyer farm, and an earthquake was reported to have shaken the entire Miskatonic Valley, registering on the seismographic instruments of Harvard College and causing swells in the harbor at Innsmouth.

The next day Squire Sawyer Whateley registered a wedding on the official rolls of Dunwich village. He claimed to be qualified to perform the civil ceremony by virtue of his standing as Chairman of the local Selective Service Board. This claim must surely be regarded as most dubious, but while the Whateleys were not highly regarded in Dunwich, their detractors considered it the better part of valor to hold their criticism to private circumstances, and the marriage of Earl Sawyer and Zenia Whateley was thus officially recognized.

Mamie Bishop, in the meanwhile, had settled into her new home in Aylesbury and began spreading malign reports about her former lover Earl Sawyer and his new wife. Earl, she claimed, had been in league with the Whateleys all along. Her own displacement by Zenia had been only one step in the plot of Earl Sawyer and the Whateley clan to revive the evil activities that had culminated in the events of 1928. Earl and Zenia, with the collaboration of Squire Sawyer Whateley and old Zebulon Whateley, would bring about the ruination of the entire Miskatonic Valley, if left to their own devices, and perhaps might bring about a blight that would cover a far greater region.

No one paid any attention to Mamie, however. Even the other Bishops, a clan almost as numerous and widespread as the Whateleys, tended to discount Mamie's warnings as the spiteful outpourings of a woman scorned. And in any case, Mamie's dire words were pushed from the public consciousness in the month of August, 1938, when Earl Sawyer rang up Dr. Houghton on the party line telephone and summoned him to the Sawyer farm.

Zenia was in labor, and Earl, in a rare moment of concern, had decided that medical assistance was in order.

Zenia's labor was a long and difficult one. Dr. Houghton later commented that first childbirths tended to be more protracted than later deliveries, but Zenia remained in labor for seventy-two consecutive hours, and barely survived until the delivery of the child. Throughout the period of her labor there were small earth temblors centering on the Devil's Hop Yard, and Zenia, by means of a series of frantic hand motions and incoherent mewling sounds, indicated that she wished the curtains drawn back from her window so that she could see the crown of the hill from her bed.

On the third night of her labor, while Zenia lay panting and spent near to death between futile contractions, a storm rose. Clouds swept up the valley from the Atlantic, great winds roared over the houses and through the trees of Dunwich, bolts of lightning flashed from thunderhead to hilltop.

Dr. Houghton, despairing of saving the life of either Zenia or her unborn child, began preparations for a caesarian section. With Earl Sawyer hovering in the background, mumbling semi-incoherent incantations of the sort that had caused the Congregational minister to refuse a church wedding to the couple, the doctor set to work.

With sharpened instruments sterilized over the woodstove that served for both cooking and heat for the Sawyer farmhouse, he made the incision in Zenia's abdomen. As he removed the fetus from her womb there was a terrific crash of thunder. A blinding bolt of lightning struck at the peak of the Devil's Hop Yard. From a small grove of twisted and deformed maple trees behind the Sawyer house, a flock of nesting whippoorwills took wing, setting up a cacophony of sound audible over even the loud rushings and pounding of the rainstorm.

All of Dr. Houghton's efforts failed to preserve the poor, limited life of Zenia Whateley Sawyer, but her child survived the ordeal of birth. The next day old Zebulon Whateley and Squire Sawyer Whateley made their way to the Sawyer house and joined Earl Sawyer in his efforts. He descended the wooden steps to the dank cellar of the house and returned carrying a plain wooden coffin that he himself had surreptitiously built some time before. The three of them placed Zenia's shriveled, wasted body in the coffin and Earl nailed its lid in place.

They carried the wooden box to the peak of the Devil's Hop Yard and there, amid fearsome incantations and the making of signs with their hands unlike any seen for a decade in the Miskatonic Valley, they buried Zenia's remains.

Then they returned to the farmhouse where the child lay in a crude wooden cradle. Squire Whateley tended the infant while its father rang up Central on the party line and placed a call to Mamie Bishop at the rooming house in Aylesbury.

After a brief conversation with his former common-law wife, Earl Sawyer nodded to his father-in-law and to the Squire, and left them with the child. He climbed into his Model T and set out along the Aylesbury Pike to fetch Mamie back to Dunwich.

★   ★   ★

The child of Earl Sawyer and Zenia Whateley Sawyer was a girl. Her father, after consultation with his father-in-law and distant cousin Squire Whateley, named his daughter Hester Sawyer. She was a tiny child at birth, and fear was expressed as to her own survival.

Earl contacted the Congregational minister at Arkham, asking him to baptize the infant according to rites specified by Earl. Once more the dispute as to the use of Earl's strange scriptures — if they could be so defined — erupted, and once more the minister refused to lend his ecclesiastical legitimacy to the ceremony. Instead, Earl, Zebulon and Sawyer Whateley carried the tiny form, wrapped in swaddling cloths, to the peak of the Devil's Hop Yard, and on the very ground of her mother's still-fresh grave conducted a ceremony of consecration best left undescribed.

They then returned her to the Sawyer house and the care of Mamie Bishop.

There were comments in Dunwich and even in Aylesbury about Mamie's surprising willingness to return to Sawyer's ménage in the role of nursemaid and guardian to the infant Hester, but Mamie merely said that she had her reasons and refused to discuss the matter further. Under Mamie's ministrations the infant Hester survived the crises of her first days of life, and developed into a child of surprising strength and precocity.

Even as an infant Hester was a child of unusual beauty and — if such a phrase may be used — premature maturity. Her coloring was fair — almost, but not quite, to the point of albinism. Where Hester's distant relative, the long-disappeared Lavinia Whateley, had had crinkly white hair and reddish-pink eyes, little Hester possessed from the day of her birth a glossy poll of the silvery blonde shade known as platinum. Mamie Bishop tried repeatedly to put up the child's hair in miniature curls or scallops as she thought appropriate for a little girl, but Hester's hair hung straight and gracefully to her shoulders, refusing to lie in any other fashion.

The child's eyes showed a flecked pattern of palest blue and the faint pink of the true albino, giving the appearance of being a pale lavender in tint except at a very close range, when the alternation of blue and pink became visible. Her skin was the shade of new cream and was absolutely flawless.

She took her first steps at the age of five months; by this time she had her full complement of baby teeth as well. By the age of eight months, early in the spring of 1939, she began to speak. There was none of the babyish prattle of a normally developing child; Hester spoke with precision, correctness, and a chilling solemnity from the utterance of her first word.

Earl Sawyer did not keep Mamie Bishop imprisoned in his house as he had the dead Zenia Whateley Sawyer. Indeed, Earl made it his business to teach Mamie the operation of his Model T, and he encouraged her — nay, he all but commanded her — to drive it into Dunwich village, Dean's Corners, or Aylesbury frequently.

On these occasions Mamie was alleged to be shopping for such necessities for herself, Earl, or little Hester as the farm did not provide. On one occasion Earl directed Mamie to drive the Model T all the way to Arkham, and there to spend three days obtaining certain items which he said were needed for Hester's upbringing. Mamie spent two nights at one of the rundown hotels that still persisted in Arkham, shabby ornate reminders of that city's more prosperous days.

Mamie's sharp tongue had its opportunities during these shopping expeditions, and she was heard frequently to utter harsh comments about Earl, Zebulon, and Squire Whateley. She never made direct reference to the dead Zenia, but uttered cryptic and unsettling remarks about little Hester Sawyer, her charge, whom she referred to most often as 'Zenia's white brat.'

As has been mentioned, Dunwich village supported no regular newspaper of its own, but the publications of other communities in the Miskatonic Valley gave space to events in this locale. The Aylesbury *Transcript* in particular devoted a column in its weekly pages to news from Dunwich. This news was provided by Joe Osborn, the proprietor of Osborn's General Store, in return for regular advertisement of his establishment's wares.

A review of the Dunwich column in the Aylesbury *Transcript* for the period between August of 1938 and the end of April of 1943 shows a series of reports of rumblings, crackings, and unpleasant odors emanating from the area of Sawyer's farm, and particularly from the Devil's Hop Yard. Two features of these reports are worthy of note.

First, the reports of the sounds and odors occur at irregular intervals, but a check of the sales records of the establishments in Dunwich, Aylesbury, Dean's Corners and Arkham where Mamie Bishop traded, will show that the occurrences at the Devil's Hop Yard coincide perfectly with the occasions of Mamie's absence from Sawyer's farm. Second, while the events took place at irregular intervals, ranging from as close together as twice in one week to as far apart as eight months, their severity increased steadily. The earliest of the series are barely noted in the Dunwich column of the *Transcript*. By the end of 1941 the events receive lead position in Osborn's writings. By the beginning of 1943 they are no longer relegated to the Dunwich column at all, but are treated as regular news, suggesting that they could be detected in Aylesbury itself — a distance of nearly fifteen miles from Dunwich.

It was also noted by the loafers at Osborn's store that on those occasions when Mamie Bishop absented herself from the Sawyer farm, Earl's two favorite in-laws and cronies, Zebulon Whateley and Squire Sawyer Whateley, visited him. There were no further reports of odd goings-on at the Sawyer place such as that made by Luther Brown in 1938.

Perhaps Luther's unfortunate demise in an accident on George Corey's silo roof, where he was placing new shingles, had no connection with his seeing the rites atop the Devil's Hop Yard, but after Luther's death and with the new series of rumblings and stenches, others began to shun the Sawyer place from 1939 onward.

In September of 1942 a sad incident transpired. Hester Sawyer, then aged four, had been educated up to that time primarily by her father, with the assistance of the two elder Whateleys and of Mamie Bishop. She had never been away from the Sawyer farm and had never seen another child.

Mamie Bishop's second cousin Elsie, the maiden sister of Silas Bishop (of the undecayed Bishops), caught Mamie's ear on one of Mamie's shopping expeditions away from the Sawyer place. Elsie was the mistress of a nursery school operated under the auspices of the Dunwich Congregational Church, and she somehow convinced Mamie that it was her duty to give little Hester exposure to other children of her own age. Mamie spoke disparagingly of 'Zenia's white brat,' but following Elsie's insistence Mamie agreed to discuss the matter with Earl Sawyer.

On the first day of the fall term, Mamie drove Earl's Model T into Dunwich village, little Hester perched on the seat beside her. This was the first look that Hester had at Dunwich — and the first that Dunwich had at Hester.

Although Mamie had bundled the child into loose garments that covered her from neck to ankles, it was obvious that something was abnormal about her. Hester was astonishingly small for a child of four. She was hardly taller than a normal infant. It was as if she had remained the same size in the four years since her birth, not increasing an inch in stature.

But that was only half the strangeness of Hester's appearance, for while her size was the same as a new-born infant's, her development was that of a fully mature and breathtakingly beautiful woman. The sun shone brilliantly on the long platinum hair that hung defiantly around the edges of the bonnet Mamie had forced onto Hester's head. Her strange lavender eyes seemed to hold secrets. Her face was mature. And when a sudden gust of wind pressed her baggy dress against her torso this revealed the configuration of a Grecian eidolon.

The loafers at Osborn's, who had clustered about and craned their necks for a look at the mysterious 'white brat' were torn between an impulse to turn away from this unnatural sight and a fascination with the image of what seemed a living manikin, a woman of voluptuous bodily form and astonishing facial beauty, the size of a day-old infant, sitting primly beside Mamie Bishop.

Elsie Bishop welcomed her cousin Mamie and her charge, Hester Sawyer, to the nursery school at the Congregational

Church. Elsie chose to make no comment on Hester's unusual appearance, but instead introduced her to the children already present. These included her own nephew Nahum Bishop, Silas's five-year-old son. Nahum was a perfectly normal boy, outgoing and playful, one of the few such to appear in the blighted Miskatonic Valley.

He took one look at Hester Sawyer and fell madly in love with her, with the total, enraptured fascination that only a child can feel when first he discovers the magic of the female sex. He lost all interest in the other children in the school and in their games. He wished only to be with Hester, to gaze at her, to hold her miniature woman's hand in his own pudgy boy's fingers. Any word that Hester spoke was as music to his ears, and any favor she might ask, any task that she might set for him, was his bounden duty and his greatest joy to perform.

In a short while the various children of the nursery school were playing happily, some of them scampering up and down the aisle leading between the two banks of pews in the main body of the church. The two cousins, Mamie and Elsie, retired to the chancel kitchen to prepare a pot of tea for themselves. Although they could not see the school children from this position, they could hear them happily playing in the semi-abandoned church.

Suddenly there was a terrible thump from the roof of the church, then a second similar sound from the burying-ground outside, then a series of panic-stricken and terrified screams from the children. Mamie and Elsie ran from the chancel and found nothing, apparently, amiss in the church itself, but the children were clustered at an open window staring into the churchyard, pointing and exclaiming in distress.

The two women shoved their way through the panic-stricken children until they could see. What they beheld was the body of Elsie's nephew Nahum Bishop, grotesquely broken over an old tomb-stone upon which it had fallen when it bounced from the roof of the church. There was no question that the child was dead, the sightless eyes apparently gazing upward at the steeple of the church.

Before they could even turn away from the window, the two women were able to hear a light tread, one so light that, except for the total hush that had descended upon the church as the children's screams subsided, it would not have been heard at all, calmly descending the wooden staircase from the steeple. In a moment Hester Sawyer emerged from the stairwell, her manner one of complete self-possession, the expression on her beautiful little face one of mockery and amusement.

When the state police arrived Hester explained, with total self-assurance, that she and Nahum had climbed the steeple together, up the narrow wooden staircase that ran from the church's floor to its belfry. Nahum had averred that he would do anything to prove his love for Hester, and she had asked him to fly from the steeple. In attempting to do so he had fallen to the roof, bounced once, then crashed onto the old grave marker in the yard.

The police report listed Nahum's death

as accidental, and Hester was returned to the Sawyer farm in the charge of Mamie Bishop. Needless to say, the child did not return to the nursery school at the Dunwich Congregational Church; in fact, she was not seen again in Dunwich, or anywhere else away from her father's holdings.

★ ★ ★

The final chapter in the tragedy of the Devil's Hop Yard, if indeed tragedy is the proper designation for such a drama, was played out in the spring of 1943. As in so many years past, the warmth of the equinox had given but little of itself to the upper Miskatonic Valley; winter instead still clung to the barren peaks and the infertile bottomlands of the region, and the icy dark waters of the Miskatonic River passed only few meadows on their way southeasterward to Arkham and Innsmouth and the cold Atlantic beyond.

In Dunwich the bereaved Silas Bishop and his maiden sister Elsie had recovered as best they could from the death of young Nahum. Elsie's work with the nursery school continued and only the boarding-up of the stairwell that led to the steeple and belfry of the Congregational Church testified to the accident of the previous September.

Early on the evening of April 30 the telephone rang in the Bishop house in Dunwich village, and Elsie lifted the receiver to hear a furtive whisper on the line. The voice she barely recognized, so distorted it was with terror, belonged to her second cousin Mamie.

'They've locked me in the house naow,' Mamie whispered into the telephone. 'Earl always sent me away before, but this time they've locked me in and I'm afeared. Help me, Elsie! I daon't knaow what they're a-fixin' ta do up ta the Hop Yard, but I'm afeared!'

Elsie signaled her brother Silas to listen to the conversation. 'Who's locked you in, Mamie?' Elsie asked her cousin.

'Earl and Zeb and Sawyer Whateley done it! They've took Zenia's brat and they've clumb the Hop Yard. I kin see 'em from here! They're all stark naked and they've built 'em a bonfire and an altar and they're throwin' powder into the fire and old Zeb he's a-readin' things outen some terrible book that they always keep a-locked up!

'And now I kin see little Hester, the little white brat o' Zenia's, and she's clumb onto the altar and she's sayin' things to Zeb an' Earl and Squire Whateley an' they've got down on their knees like they's a-worshippin' Hester, and she's makin' signs with her hands. Oh, Elsie, I can't describe them signs, they's so awful, they's so awful what she's a-doin', Elsie! Get some help out here, oh, please get some help!'

Elsie told Mamie to try and be calm, and not to watch what was happening atop the Devil's Hop Yard. Then she hung up the telephone and turned to her brother Silas. 'We'll get the state police from Aylesbury,' she said. 'They'll stop whatever is happening at Sawyer's. We'd best telephone them now, Silas!'

'D'ye think they'll believe ye, Elsie?'

Elsie shook her head in a negative manner.

'Then we'd best git to Aylesbury ourselves,' Silas resumed. 'If we go there ourselves they'd more like to believe us than if we jest telephoned.'

They hitched up their horse and drove by wagon from Dunwich to Aylesbury. Fortunately the state police officer who had investigated the death of young Nahum Bishop was present, and knowing both Elsie and Silas to be citizens of a responsible nature the officer did not laugh at their report of Mamie's frightened telephone call. The officer started an automobile belonging to the state police, and with the two Bishops as passengers set out back along the Aylesbury Pike to Dunwich, and thence to the Sawyer farm beyond the village center.

As the official vehicle neared Sawyer's place, its three occupants were assailed by a most terrible and utterly indescribable stench that turned their stomachs and caused their eyes to run copiously, and that also, inexplicably, filled each of them with a hugely frightening rush of emotions dominated by an amalgam of fear and revulsion. Sounds of thunder filled the air, and the earth trembled repeatedly, threatening to throw the car off the road.

The state police officer swung the automobile from the dirt road fronting the Sawyer farm onto a narrow and rutted track that ran by the decrepit house and led to the foot of the Devil's Hop Yard. The officer pulled the car to a halt and leaped from its seat, charging up the hill with his service revolver drawn, followed by Silas and Elsie Bishop, who made the best speed they could despite their years.

Before them they could see the altar and the four figures that Mamie Bishop had described to her cousin Elsie. The night sky was cloudless and a new moon offered no competition to the millions of brilliantly twinkling stars. Little Hester Sawyer, her body that of a fully formed woman yet not two feet in height, danced and postured on the wooden altar, the starlight and that of the nearby bonfire dancing on her gleaming platinum hair and smooth, cream-colored skin. Her lavender eyes caught the firelight and reflected it like the eyes of a wild beast in the woods at night.

Earl and Zebulon and Sawyer Whateley stood in an equilateral triangle about the altar, and around them there had apparently sprung from the earth itself a perfect circle of slimy, tentacled growths, more animal than vegetable, the only things that had ever been known to grow from the soil of the Devil's Hop Yard. Even as the newcomers watched, too awe-stricken and too revolted to act, the horrid tentacled growths began to lengthen, and to sway in time to the awful chanting of the three naked men and the posturings of the tiny, four-year-old Hester.

There was the sound of a shrill, reedy piping from somewhere in the air, and strange winds rushed back and forth over the scene.

The voice of Hester Sawyer could be heard chanting, '*Ygnaith . . . ygnaith . . . thflthkh 'ngha . . . Yog-Sothoth . . . Y'bthnk . . . h'ehye-n'grkdl'lh!*'

There was a single, blinding bolt of lightning — an astonishing occurrence as the night sky was entirely clear of any clouds — and the form of Hester Sawyer was bathed in a greenish-yellow glow of almost supernatural electrical display, sparks dancing over her perfect skin, and balls of St. Elmo's fire tumbling from her lips and hands and rolling across the altar, tumbling to the ground and bounding down the slopes of the Devil's Hop Yard.

The eyes of the watchers were so dazzled by the display that they were never certain, afterwards, of what they had seen. But it appeared, at least, that the bolt of lightning had not descended from the sky to strike Hester, but had *originated from her* and struck upward, zigzagging into the wind-swept blackness over Dunwich, streaking upward and upward as if it were eventually going to reach the stars themselves.

And even more quickly than the bolt of lightning had disappeared from before the dazzled eyes of the watchers, the body of Hester Sawyer appeared to rise along its course, posturing and making those terrible shocking signs even as it rose, growing ever smaller as it disappeared above the Hop Yard until the lightning bolt winked out and all sight of Hester Sawyer was lost forever.

With the end of the electrical display the shocked paralysis that had overcome the watchers subsided, and the police officer advanced to stand near the ring of tentacled growths and the three naked men. He ordered them to follow him back to the police vehicle, but instead they launched themselves in snarling, animalistic attacks upon him. The officer stepped back but the three men flew at him growling, clawing, biting at his legs and torso. The police officer's revolver crashed once, again, then a third time, and the three naked men lay thrashing and gesturing on the ground.

They were taken to the general hospital at Arkham, where a medical team headed by Drs. Houghton and Hartwell labored unsuccessfully through the night to save them. By the morning of May 1, all three had expired without uttering a single word.

Meanwhile, back at the Devil's Hop

Yard, Silas and Elsie Bishop guided other investigators to the altar that Hester Sawyer had last stood upon. The book that had lain open beside her had been destroyed beyond identification by the lightning bolt of the night of April 30. Agricultural experts summoned from Miskatonic University at Arkham attempted to identify the tentacled growths that had sprung from the ground around the altar. The growths had died within a few hours of their appearance, and only desiccated husks remained. The experts were unable to identify them fully, indicating their complete puzzlement at their apparent resemblance to the tentacles of the giant marine squid of the Pacific Trench near the island of Ponape.

Back at the Sawyer farmhouse, Mamie Bishop was found cowering in a corner, hiding her eyes and refusing to look up or even acknowledge the presence of others when addressed. Her hair had turned completely white; not the platinum white of little Hester Sawyer's hair but the crinkly albino white that had been Lavinia Whateley's so many years before.

Mamie mumbled to herself and shook her head but uttered not a single intelligible word, either then or later, when she too was taken to the general hospital at Arkham. In time she was certified physically sound and transferred to a mental ward where she resides to this day, a harmless, quivering husk, her inward-turned eyes locked forever on whatever shocking sight it was that she beheld that night when she gazed from the window of the Sawyer farmhouse upon the horrid ceremony taking place atop the Devil's Hop Yard.

Documents In The Case
Of Elizabeth Akeley

Surveillance of the Spiritual Light Brother-hood Church of San Diego was initiated as a result of certain events of the mid and late 1970s.

Great controversy had arisen over the conduct of the followers of the Guru Maharaj-ji, the International Society for Krishna Consciousness (the 'Hare Krish-nas'), the Church of Scientology, and the Unification Church headed by the Rever-end Sun Myung Moon. These activities were cloaked in the Constitutional shield of 'freedom of religion,' and the cults for the most part resisted suggestions of investigation by grand juries or other official bodies.

Even so, the tragic events concerning the People's Temple of San Francisco aroused government concern which could not be stymied. While debate raged publicly over the question of opening cult records, Federal and local law enforcement agencies covertly entered the field.

It was within this context that interest was aroused concerning the operation of the Spiritual Light Brotherhood, and particularly its leader, the Radiant Mother Elizabeth Akeley.

Outwardly there was nothing secret in the operation of Mother Akeley's church. The group operated from a building located at the corner of Second Street and Ash in a neighborhood described as 'genteel shabby,' midway between the commercial center of San Diego and the city's tourist-oriented waterfront area.

The building occupied by the Church had been erected originally by a more conventional denomination, but the vicissitudes of shifting population caused the building to be deconsecrated and sold to the Spiritual Light Brotherhood. The new owners, led by their order's founder and then-leader, the Radiant Father George Goodenough Akeley, clearly marked the building with its new identity.

The headline was changed on the

church's bulletin board, and the symbol of the Spiritual Light Brotherhood, a shining tetrahedron of neon tubing, was erected atop the steeple. A worship service was held each Sunday morning, and a spiritual message service was conducted each Wednesday evening.

In later years, following the death of the Radiant Father in 1970 and the accession to leadership of the Church by Elizabeth Akeley, Church archives were maintained in the form of tape recordings. The Sunday services were apparently a bland amalgam of non-denominational Judeo-Christian teachings, half-baked and quarter-understood Oriental mysticism, and citations from the works of Einstein, Heisenberg, Shklovskii, and Fermi.

Surviving cassettes of the Wednesday message services are similarly innocuous. Congregants were invited to submit questions or requests for messages from deceased relatives. The Radiant Mother accepted a limited number of such requests at each service. The congregants would arrange themselves in a circle and link their fingers in the classic manner of participants in séances. Mother Akeley would enter a trance and proceed to answer the questions or deliver messages from the deceased, 'as the spirits moved her.'

Audioanalysis of the tapes of these séances indicates that, while the intonation and accent of the voices varied greatly, from the whines and lisps of small children to the quaverings of the superannuated, and from the softened and westernized pronunciations of native San Diegans to the harsh and barbaric tones of their New Yorker parents, the vocal apparatus was at all times that of Elizabeth Akeley. The variations were no greater than those attainable by an actress of professional training or natural brilliance.

Such, however, was not the case with a startling portion of the cassette for the session of Wednesday, June 13, 1979. The Radiant Mother asked her congregants if anyone had a question for the spirits, or if any person present wished to attempt contact with some deceased individual.

A number of questions were answered,

dealing with the usual matters of marriage and divorce, reassurances of improved health, and counseling as to investments and careers.

An elderly congregant who was present stated that her husband had died the previous week, and she sought affirmation of his happiness 'on the other side.'

The Radiant Mother moaned. Then she muttered incoherently. All of this was as usual at the beginning of her trances. Shortly the medium's vocal quality altered. Her normally soft, rather pleasant and distinctly feminine voice dropped in register until it suggested that of a man. Simultaneously, her contemporary Californian diction turned to the twang of a rural New Englander.

While the sound quality of this tape is excellent, the medium's diction was unfortunately not so. The resulting record is necessarily fragmentary. As nearly as it has been transcribed, this is it:

'Wilmarth . . . Wilmarth . . . back. Have come . . . Antares . . . Neptune, Pluto, Yuggoth. Yes, Wilmarth. Yug —

'Are you . . . If I cannot receive

. . . Windham County . . . yes, Townshend . . . round hill. Wilmarth still alive? Then who . . . son, son . . .

' . . . ever receives . . . communicate enough Akeley, 176 Pleasant . . . go, California. Son, see if you can find my old friend Albert Wilmarth . . . chusetts . . .

'With wings. Twisted ropes for heads and blood like plant sap . . . Flying, flying, and all the while a gramophone recordi . . . must apologize to Wilmarth if he's still alive, but I also have the most wonderful news, the most wonderful tales to tell him . . .

' . . . and its smaller satellites, well, I don't suppose anyone will believe me, of course, but not only is Yuggoth there, revolving regularly except in an orbit at right angles to the plane of the ecliptic, no wonder no one believed in it, but what I must describe to you, Albert, the planet glows with a heat and a demoniacal ruby glare that illuminates its own . . . thon and Zaman, Thog and Thok, I could hardly believe my own . . .

' . . . goid beings who cannot . . . corporeally . . . Neptune . . . central caverns of a dark star beyond the rim of the galaxy its . . .

' . . . wouldn't call her beautiful, of course . . . dinary terms . . . than an arachnid and a cetacean, and yet, could a spider and dolphin by some miracle establish mental communion, who knows what . . . not really a name as you normally think of names, but . . . Sh'ch'rru'a . . . of Aldebaran, the eleventh, has a constellation of inhabited moons, which . . . independently, or perhaps at some earlier time, travelling by means simi . . .

' . . . ummate in metal cannisters, will be necessary to . . . aid in obtaining . . . fair exchange, for the donors will receive a far greater boon in the form . . . '

At this point the vocal coherence, such as it is, breaks down. The male voice with its New England twang cracks and rises in tone even as the words are replaced by undecipherable mumbles. Mother Akeley recovers from her trance state, and the séance draws quickly to a close. From the internal evidence of the contents of the tape, the Radiant Mother had no awareness of the message, or narration, delivered by the male voice speaking through her. This also is regarded, among psychic and spiritualistic circles, as quite the usual state of affairs with trance mediums.

★ ★ ★

Authorities next became aware of unusual activities through a copy of the *Vermont Unidentified Flying Object Intelligencer*, or *Vufoi*. Using a variety of the customary cover names and addresses for the purpose, such Federal agencies as the FBI, NSA, Department of Defense, NASA, and National Atmospheric and Oceanographic Agency subscribe regularly to publications of organizations like the Vermont UFO Intelligence Bureau and other self-appointed investigatory bodies.

The President of the Vermont UFO Intelligence Bureau and editor of its *Intelligencer* was identified as one Ezra Noyes. Noyes was known to reside with his parents (Ezra was nineteen years of age at the time) in the community of Dark Mountain, Windham County. Noyes customarily prepared *Vufoi* issues himself, assembling material both from outside sources and from members of the Vermont UFO Intelligence Bureau, most of whom were former high school friends now employed by local merchants or farmers, or attending Windham County Community College in Townshend.

Noyes would assemble his copy, type it onto mimeograph stencils using a portable machine set up on the kitchen table, and run off copies on a superannuated mimeograph kept beside the washer and dryer in the basement. The last two items prepared for each issue were 'Vufoi Voice' and 'From the Editor's Observatory,' commenting in one case flippantly and in the other seriously, on the contents of the issue. 'Vufoi Voice' was customarily illustrated with a crude cartoon of a man wearing an astronaut's headgear, and was signed 'Cap'n Oof-oh.' 'From the Editor's Observatory' was illustrated with a drawing of an astronomical telescope with a tiny figure seated at the eyepiece, and was signed 'Intelligencer.'

It is believed that both 'Cap'n Oof-oh' and 'Intelligencer' were Ezra Noyes.

The issue of the *Vermont Unidentified Flying Object Intelligencer* for June 1979 actually appeared early in August of that year. Excerpts from the two noted columns follow:

From the Editor's Observatory

Of greatest interest since our last issue — and we apologize for missing the March, April and May editions due to unavoidable circumstances — has been the large number of organic sightings here in the northern Vermont region. We cannot help but draw similes to the infamous Colorado cattle mutilizations of the past year or few years, and the ill-conceived Air Farce cover-up efforts *which only draw extra attention to the facts that they can't hide from us who know the Truth!*

Local historians like Mr. Littleton at the High School remember other incidents and the Brattleboro *Reformer* and Arkham *Advertiser* and other Newspapers whose back files constitute an Official Public Record could tell the story of other incidents like this one! It is hard to reconciliate the Windham County sightings and the Colorado Cattle Mutiliation Case with others such as the well-known Moth Man sightings in the Southland and especially the Bat-wing creature sightings of as long as a half of a century ago but with a sufficient ingeniusity it is definitely not a task beyond undertaking and the U.S. Air Farce and other cover-up agencies are hear-bye placed on Official notice that such is our intention and we will not give up until success is ours and the cover-up is blown as Sky-High as the UFO sightings themselves!

Yours until our July issue,
Intelligencer.

Vufoi Voice
Bat-wing and Moth Man indeed! Didn't I read something like that in

Detective Comics back when Steve Englehart was writing for DC? Or was it in *Mad*? Come to think of it, when it's hard to tell the parody from the original, things are gettin' *mighty* strange.

And there gettin' mighty strange around here!

We wonder what the ole Intelligencer's been smoking in that smelly meerschaum he affects around Intelligence Bureau meetings. Could it be something illegal that he grows for himself up on the mountainside?

Or is he just playing Sherlock Holmes?

We ain't impressed.

Impressionable, yep! My mom always said I was impressionable as a boy, back on the old asteroid farm in Beta Reticuli, but this is too silly for words.

Besides, she tuck me to the eye dock and he fitted us out with a pair of gen-yew-ine X-ray specs, and that not only cured us of Reticule-eye but now we can see right through such silliness as bat-winged moth men carrying silvery cannisters around the skies and the hillsides with 'em.

Shades of a Japanese Sci-Fi Flick! This musta been the stuntman out for lunch!

And that's where we think the old Intelligencer is this month: *Out 2 Lunch*!

Speaking of which, I haven't had mine yet this afternoon, and if I don't hurry up and have it pretty soon it'll be time for dinner and then I'll have to eat my lunch for a bedtime snack and that'll confuse the dickens out of my poor stomach! So I'm off to hit the old fridgidaire (not too hard, I don't want to spoil the shiny finish on my new spaceman's gloves!), and I'll see you-all nextish!

Whoops, here's our saucer now! Bye-bye,

Cap'n Oof-oh.

★　★　★

Following the extraordinary spiritual message service of June 13, Mother Akeley was driven to her home at 176 Pleasant Street in National City, a residential suburb of San Diego, by her boyfriend, Marc Feinman.

Investigation revealed that she had met

Feinman casually while sunning herself and watching the surfers ride the waves in at Black's Beach, San Diego. Shortly thereafter, Elizabeth had been invited by a female friend of approximately her own age to attend a concert given by a musical group, a member of which was a friend of Akeley's friend. Outside of her official duties as Radiant Mother of the Spiritual Light Brotherhood, Elizabeth Akeley was known to live quite a normal life for a young woman of her social and economic class.

She accompanied her friend to the concert, visited the backstage area with her, and was introduced to the musician. He in turn introduced Elizabeth to other members of the musical group, one of whom Elizabeth recognized as her casual acquaintance of Black's Beach. A further relationship developed, in which it was known that Akeley and Feinman frequently exchanged overnight visits. Elizabeth had retained the house on Pleasant Street originally constructed by her grandfather, George Goodenough Akeley, when he had emigrated to San

Diego from Vermont in the early 1920s.

Marc had been born and raised in the Bronx, New York, had emigrated to the West Coast following his college years and presently resided in a pleasant apartment on Upas Street near Balboa Park. From here he commuted daily to his job as a computer systems programmer in downtown San Diego, his work as a musician being more of an avocation than a profession.

On Sunday, June 17, for the morning worship service of the Spiritual Light Brotherhood, Radiant Mother Akeley devoted her sermon to the previous Wednesday's séance, an unusual practice for her. The sexton of the church, a nondescript-looking black man named Vernon Whiteside, attended the service. Noting the Radiant Mother's departure from her usual bland themes, Whiteside communicated with the Federal Agency which had infiltrated him into the Church for precisely this purpose. An investigation of Mother Akeley's background was then initiated.

Within a short time, Agent Whiteside

was in possession of a preliminary report on Elizabeth Akeley and her forebears, excerpts from which follow.

AKELEY, ELIZABETH — HISTORY AND BACKGROUND

The Akeley family is traceable to one *Beelzebub Akeley* who traveled from Portsmouth, England, to Kingsport, Massachusetts aboard the sailing caravel *Worthy* in 1607. Beelzebub Akeley married an indentured servant girl, bought out her indenture papers and moved with her to establish the Akeley dynasty in Townshend, Windham County, Vermont in 1618. The Akeleys persisted in Windham County for more than two centuries, producing numerous clergy, academics, and other genteel professionals in this period.

Abednego Mesach Akeley, subject's great-great grandfather, was the last of the Vermont Akeleys to pursue a life of the cloth. Born in 1832, Abednego was raised in the strict puritanical traditions of the Akeleys and ordained by his father, the Reverend *Samuel Shadrach Solomon Akeley* upon attaining his maturity. Abednego served as assistant pastor to his father until Samuel's death in 1868, at which time he succeeded to the pulpit.

Directly following the funeral of Samuel Akeley, Abednego is known to have traveled to more southerly regions of New England, including Massachusetts and possibly Rhode Island. Upon his return to Townshend he led his flock into realms of highly questionable doctrine, and actually transferred the affiliation of his church from its traditional Protestant parent body to that of the new and suspect Starry Wisdom sect.

Controversy and scandal followed at once, and upon the death of Abednego early in 1871 at the age of thirty-nine, the remnants of his congregation moved as a body to Providence, Rhode Island. One female congregant, however, was excommunicated by unanimous vote of the other members of the congregation, and forced to remain behind in Townshend. This female was *Sarah*

Elizabeth Phillips, a servant girl in the now defunct Akeley household.

Shortly following the departure of the remnants of Abednego Akeley's flock from Vermont, Sarah Phillips gave birth to a son. She claimed that the child had been fathered by Abednego mere hours before his death. She named the child *Henry Wentworth Akeley*. As the Akeley clan was otherwise extinct at this point, no one challenged Sarah's right to identify her son as an Akeley, and in fact in later years she sometimes used the name Akeley herself.

Henry Akeley overcame his somewhat shadowed origins and built for himself a successful academic career, returning to Windham County in his retirement, and remaining there until the time of his mysterious disappearance and presumed demise in the year 1928.

Henry had married some years earlier, and his wife had given birth to a single child, *George Goodenough Akeley*, in the year 1901, succumbing two days later to childbed fever. Henry Akeley raised his son with the assistance of a series of nursemaids and housekeepers. At the time of Henry Akeley's retirement and his return to Townshend, George Akeley emigrated to San Diego, California, building there a modest but comfortable house at 176 Pleasant Street.

George Akeley married a local woman suspected of harboring a strain of Indian blood; the George Akeleys were the parents of a set of quadruplets born in 1930. This was the first quadruple birth on record in San Diego County. There were three boys and a girl. The boys seemed, at birth, to be of relatively robust constitution, although naturally small. The girl was still smaller, and seemed extremely feeble at birth so that her survival appeared unlikely.

However, with each passing hour the boys seemed to fade while the tiny girl grew stronger. All four infants clung tenaciously to life, the boys more and more weakly and the girl more strongly, until finally the three male infants — apparently at the same hour — succumbed. The girl took nourishment with enthusiasm, growing pink and active.

Her spindly limbs rounded into healthy baby arms and legs, and in due course she was carried from the hospital by her father.

In honor of a leading evangelist of the era, and of a crusader for spiritualistic causes, the girl was named *Aimee Semple Conan Doyle Akeley*.

Aimee traveled between San Diego and the spiritualist center of Noblesville, Indiana, with her parents. The George Akeleys spent their winters in San Diego, where George Goodenough Akeley served as Radiant Father of the Spiritual Light Brotherhood, which he founded in a burst of religious fervor after meeting Aimee Semple McPherson, the evangelist whose name his daughter bore; each summer they would make a spiritualistic pilgrimage to Noblesville, where George Akeley became fast friends with the spiritualist leader and sometime American fascist, *William Dudley Pelley*.

Aimee Doyle Akeley married William Pelley's nephew *Hiram Wesley Pelley* in 1959. In that same year Aimee's mother died and was buried in Noblesville. Her father continued his ministry in San Diego.

In 1961, two years after her marriage to young Pelley, Aimee Doyle Akeley Pelley gave birth to a daughter who was named *Elizabeth Maude Pelley*, after two right-wing political leaders, Elizabeth Dilling of Illinois and Maude Howe of England. Elizabeth Maude Pelley was raised alternately by her parents in Indiana and her grandfather in San Diego.

In San Diego her life was relatively normal, centering on her schooling, her home, and to a lesser extent on her grandfather's church, the Spiritual Light Brotherhood. In Indiana she was exposed to a good deal of political activity of a right-wing extremist nature. Hiram Wesley Pelley had followed in his uncle's footsteps in this regard, and Aimee Semple Conan Doyle Akeley Pelley took her lead from her husband and his family. A number of violent scenes are reported to have transpired between young Elizabeth Pelley and the elder Pelleys.

Elizabeth Pelley broke with her parents over political disagreements in 1976, and returned permanently to San Diego where she took up residence with her grandfather. At this time she abandoned her mother's married name and took the family name as her own, henceforth being known as *Elizabeth Akeley*. Upon the death of George Goodenough Akeley, Elizabeth succeeded to the title of Radiant Mother of the Spiritual Light Brotherhood and the pastorhood of the Church, as well as the property on Pleasant Street and a small income from inherited securities.

★ ★ ★

Vernon Whiteside read the report carefully. Through his position as sexton of the Spiritual Light Brotherhood Church he had access, as well, to most church records, including the taped archives of the Sunday worship services and Wednesday message services. He followed the Radiant Mother's report to the congregation, in which she referred heavily to the séance of June 13, by borrowing and listening carefully to the tape of the séance itself.

He also obtained a photocopy from Agency headquarters, of the latest issues of the *Vermont UFO Intelligencer*. These he read carefully, seeking to correlate any references in the newsletter with the Akeley family, or with any other name connected with the Akeleys or the content of the séance tape. He mulled over the Akeleys, Phillipses, Wilmarths, Noyeses, and all other references. He attempted also to connect the defunct (or at least seemingly-defunct) Starry Wisdom sect of the New England region, with the San Diego-based Spiritual Light Brotherhood.

At this time it appears also that Elizabeth Akeley began to receive additional messages outside of the Spiritual Light message services. During quiet moments she would lapse involuntarily into her trance or trance-like state. Because she was unable to recall the messages received during these episodes, she prevailed upon Marc Feinman to spend increasing amounts of time with her. During the last week of June and July of 1979 the two were nearly inseparable.

They spent every night together, sometimes at Elizabeth's house in National City, sometimes at Marc's apartment on Upas Street.

It was at this time that Vernon Whiteside recommended that Agency surveillance of the San Diego cult be increased by the installation of wiretaps on the church and the Pleasant Street and Upas Street residences. This recommendation was approved and recordings were obtained at all three locations. Transcripts are available in Agency files. Excerpts follow:

July 25, 1979 (Incoming)
Voice #1 (Definitely identified as Marc Feinman): Hello.
Voice #2 (Tentatively identified as Mrs. Sara Feinman, Marc's mother, Bronx, New York): Marc.
Voice #1: (Pause.) Yes, Ma.
Voice #2: Markie, are you all right?
Voice #1: Yeah, Ma.
Voice #2: Are you sure? Are you really all right?
Voice #1: Ma, I'm all right.

Voice #2: Okay, just so you're all right, Markie. And work, Markie? How's your work? Is your work all right?

Voice #1: It's all right, Ma.

Voice #2: No problems?

Voice #1: Of course, problems, Ma. That's what they pay me to take care of.

Voice #2: Oh my God, Markie! What kind of problems, Markie?

Voice #1: (Pauses, sighs or inhales deeply) We're trying to integrate the 2390 remote console control routines with the sysgen status word register and every time we run it against —

Voice #2: (Interrupting) Markie, you know I don't understand that kind of —

Voice #1: (Interrupting) But you asked me —

Voice #2: (Interrupting) Marc, don't contradict your mother. Are you still with that shicksa? She's the one who's poisoning your mind against your poor mother. I'll bet she's with you now, isn't she, Marc?

Voice #1: (Sighs or inhales deeply) No, Ma, it's Wednesday. She's never here Wednesdays. She's at church every Wednesday.

They have these services every Wedn —

Voice #2: That isn't what I called about. I don't understand, Markie, for the money that car must have cost you could have had an Oldsmobile at least, even a Buick like your father. Markie, it's your father I phoned about. Markie, you have to come home. Your father isn't well, Markie. I phoned because he isn't home now but the doctor said he's not a well man. Markie, you have to come home and talk to your father. He respects you, he listens to you God knows why. Please, Markie. (Sound of soft crying.)

Voice #1 What's wrong with him, Ma?

Voice #2 I don't want to say it on the telephone.

★   ★   ★

July 25, 1979 (Outgoing)

Voice #3: (Definitely identified as Vernon Whiteside): Spiritual Light Brotherhood. May the divine light shine upon your path.

Voice #1: Vern, this is Marc. Is Liz still at the church? Is the service over?

Voice #3: The service ended a few minutes ago, Mr. Feinman. The Radiant Mother is resting in the sacristy.

Voice #1: That's what I wanted to know. Listen, Vern, tell Lizzie that I'm on my way, will you? I had a long phone call from my mother and I don't want Liz to worry. Tell her I'll give her a ride home from the church.

★　★　★

Feinman left San Diego by automobile, driving his Ferrari Boxer eastward at a top speed in the 140 MPH range, and arrived at the home of his parents in the Bronx, New York, some time during the night of July 27–28.

In the absence of Marc Feinman, Akeley took Agent Whiteside increasingly into her confidence, asking him to remain in her presence day and night. He set up a temporary cot in the living room of the Pleasant Street house during this period. His instructions were to keep a portable cassette recorder handy at all times, and to record anything said by Mother Akeley during spontaneous trances. On the first Saturday of August, following a lengthy speech in the now-familiar male New England twang, Akeley asked Agent Whiteside for the tape. She played it back, then made the following long-distance telephone call:

August 4, 1979 (Outgoing)

Voice #4 (Tentatively identified as Ezra Noyes): Vermont Bureau. May we help you?

Voice #5 (Definitely identified as Elizabeth Akeley): Is this Mr. Noyes?

Voice #4: Oh, I'm sorry, Dad isn't home. This is Ezra. Can I give him a —

Voice #5 (Interrupting): Oh, I wanted to speak with Ezra Noyes. The editor of the *UFO Intelligencer*.

Voice #4: Oh, yes, right. Yes, that's me. Ezra Noyes.

Voice #5: Mr. Noyes, I wonder if you could help me. I need some information about, ah, recent occurrences in or around Townshend.

Voice #4: That's funny, what did you say your name was?

Voice #5: Elizabeth Akeley.

Voice #4: I thought I knew all my subbers.

Voice #5: Oh, I'm not a subscriber, I got your name from — well, that doesn't matter. Mr. Noyes, I wonder if you could tell me if there have been any unusual UFO sightings in your region lately.

Voice #4 (Suspiciously): Unusual?

Voice #5: Well, these wouldn't be your usual run-of-the-mill flying objects. Flying saucers. I hope that phrase doesn't offend you. These would be more like flying creatures.

Voice #4: Creatures? You mean birds?

Voice #5: No. No. Intelligent creatures.

Voice #4: People, then. You mean Buck Rogers and Wilma Deering with their rocket flying belts.

Voice #5. Please don't be sarcastic, Mr. Noyes. (Pauses.) I mean intelligent, possibly hominoid but non-human creatures. Their configuration may vary, but some of them, at least, I believe would have large, membranous wings, probably stretched over a bony or veinous framework in the fashion of bats' or insects'

145

wings. Also, some of them may be carrying artifacts such as polished metallic cylinders of a size capable of containing a — of containing, uh, a human — a human — brain. (Sounds of distress, possible sobbing.)

Voice #4: Miss Akeley? Are you all right, Miss Akeley?

Voice #5: I'm sorry. Yes, I'm all right.

Voice #4: I didn't mean to be so hard on you, Miss Akeley. It's just that we get a lot of crank calls. People wanting to talk to the little green men and that kind of thing. I had to make sure that you weren't —

Voice #5: I understand. And you *have* had —

Voice #4: I'm reluctant to say too much on the phone. Miss Akeley, do you think you could get here? There have been sightings. And there are older ones. Records in the local papers. A rash of incidents about fifty years ago. And others farther back. There was a monograph by an Eli Davenport over in New Hampshire back in the 1830s, I've got a Xerox of it . . .

Shortly after her telephone conversation with Ezra Noyes, Elizabeth Akeley appealed to Vernon Whiteside for assistance. 'I don't want to go alone,' she is reported as saying. 'If only Marc were here, I know he'd help me. He'd go with me. But he's with his family and I can't wait till he gets back. We'll have to close the church. No, no we won't. We can have a lay reader conduct the worship services. We can suspend the message services 'til I get back. Will you help me, Vernon?'

Whiteside, maintaining his cover as the sexton of the Brotherhood, assured Akeley. 'Anything the Radiant Mother wishes, ma'am. What would you like me to do?'

'Can you get away for a few days? I have to go to Vermont. Would you book two tickets for us? There are church funds to cover the cost.'

'Yes, ma'am.' Whiteside lowered his head. 'Best way would be via Logan International in Boston, then a Boston and Maine train to Newfane and Hardwick.'

Akeley made no comment on the sexton's surprising familiarity with transcontinental air routes or with the railroad service between Boston and upper New England. She was obviously in an agitated state, Whiteside reported when he checked in with his superiors prior to their departure from San Diego.

Two days later, the sexton and the Radiant Mother climbed down from B&M train #5508 at Hardwick, Vermont. They were met at the town's rundown and musty-smelling station by Ezra Noyes. Noyes was driving his parents' 1959 Nash Ambassador station wagon and willingly loaded Akeley's and Whiteside's meager baggage into the rear cargo deck of the vehicle.

Ezra chauffeured the visitors to his parents' home. The house, a gambrel-roofed structure of older design, was fitted for a larger family than the two senior Noyeses and their son Ezra; in fact, an elder son and daughter had both married and departed Windham County for locales of greater stimulation and professional opportunity, leaving two surplus bedrooms in the Noyes home.

Young Noyes proposed that he invite the full membership of the Vermont UFO Intelligence Bureau to attend an extraordinary meeting, to convene without delay at his home. Both Elizabeth Akeley and Vernon Whiteside demurred, pleading fatigue at the end of their transcontinental flight as well as the temporary debilitation of jet-lag.

Noyes agreed reluctantly to abandon his plan for the meeting, but was eager to offer his own services and assistance to Akeley and Whiteside. Elizabeth informed Ezra Noyes that she had received instructions to meet a visitor at a specific location near the town of Passumpsic in neighboring Caledonia County. She did not explain to Noyes the method of her receiving these instructions, but Vernon's later report indicated that he was aware of them, the instructions having been delivered to Miss Akeley in spontaneous trance sessions, the tapes of which he had also audited.

It must be again emphasized at this point that the voice heard on the spontaneous trance tapes was, in different senses, both that of Miss Akeley and of another personage. The pitch and accent, as has been stated, were those of an elderly male speaking in a semi-archaic New England twang while the vocal apparatus itself was unquestionably that of Elizabeth Akeley, neé Elizabeth Maude Pelley.

Miss Akeley's instructions were quite specific in terms of geography, although it was found odd that they referred only to landmarks and highway or road facilities known to exist in the late 1920s. Young Noyes was able to provide alternate routes for such former roadways as had been closed when superseded by more modern construction.

Before retiring, Elizabeth Akeley placed a telephone call to the home of Marc Feinman's parents in the Bronx. In this call she urged Feinman to join her in Vermont. Feinman responded that his father, at the urging of himself and his mother, had consented to undergo major surgery. Marc promised to travel to Vermont and rendezvous with Akeley at the earliest feasible time, but indicated that he felt obliged to remain with his parents until the surgery was completed and his father's recovery assured.

The following morning Elizabeth Akeley set out for Passumpsic. She was accompanied by Vernon Whiteside and traveled in the Nash Ambassador station wagon driven by Ezra Noyes.

Her instructions had contained very specific and very emphatic requirements that she keep the rendezvous alone, although others might provide transportation and wait while the meeting took place. The party who had summoned Elizabeth Akeley to the rendezvous had not, to this time, been identified, although it was believed to be the owner of the male voice and New England twang who had spoken through Elizabeth herself in her trances.

Prior to their departing Windham County for Caledonia County, a discussion took place between Akeley and Whiteside. Whiteside appealed to Elizabeth Akeley to permit him to accompany her to the rendezvous.

That would be impossible, Akeley stated.

Whiteside pointed out Elizabeth's danger, in view of the unknown identity of the other party. When Akeley remained adamant, Whiteside gave in and agreed to remain with Ezra Noyes during the meeting. It must be pointed out that at this time the dialog was not cast in the format of a highly trained and responsible agent of the Federal establishment, and an ordinary citizen; rather, the façade which Whiteside rightly although with difficulty maintained was that of a sexton of the Spiritual Light Brotherhood acting under the authority of and in the service of the Radiant Mother of the Church.

Akeley was fitted with a concealed microphone which transmitted on a frequency capable of being picked up by a small microcassette recorder which Whiteside was to keep with him in or near the Nash station wagon; additionally, an earphone ran from the recorder so that Whiteside was enabled to monitor the taped information in real time.

The Nash Ambassador crossed the county line from Windham into Caledonia on a two-lane county highway. This had been a dirt road in the 1920s, blacktopped with Federal funds administered by the Works Progress Administration under Franklin Roosevelt, and superseded by a nearby four-lane asphalt highway built during the Eisenhower Presidency. The blacktop received minimal maintenance, and only pressure from local members of the Vermont legislature, this brought in turn at the insistence of local residents who used the highway for access to Passumpsic, South Londonderry, and Bellows Falls, prevented the State from declaring the highway closed and striking it from official roadmaps.

Reaching the town of Passumpsic, Akeley, who had never previously traveled farther east than Indianapolis, Indiana, told Ezra to proceed eight hundred yards, at which point the car was to be halted. Ezra complied. At the appointed spot, Akeley left the car and opened a gate in the wooden fence fronting the highway.

Noyes pulled the wagon from the highway through the gate and found himself on a narrow track that had once been a small dirt road, long since abandoned and overgrown.

This track led away from the highway and into hilly farm country, years before abandoned by the poor farmers of the region that lay between Passumpsic and Lyndonville.

Finally, having rounded an ancient dome-topped protuberance that stood between the station wagon and any possible visual surveillance from the blacktop highway or even the overgrown dirt road, the Nash halted, unable to continue. The vegetation hereabouts was of a peculiar nature. While most of the region consisted of thin, played-out soil whose poor fertility was barely adequate to sustain a covering of tall grasses and undersized, gnarly-trunked trees, in the small area set off by the dome-topped hill the growth was thick, lush and luxuriant.

However, there was a peculiar quality to the vegetation, a characteristic which even the most learned botanist would have been hard pressed to identify, and yet which was undeniably present. It was as if the vegetation were *too* vibrantly alive, as if it sucked greedily at the earth for nourishment and by so doing robbed the countryside for a mile or more in every direction of sustenance.

Through an incongruously luxuriant copse of leafy trees a small building could be seen, clearly a shack of many years' age and equally clearly of long abandonment. The door hung angularly from a single rusted hinge, the windows were cracked or missing altogether and spiders had filled the empty frames with their own geometric handiwork. The paint, if ever the building had known the touch of a painter's brush, had long since flaked away and been blown to oblivion by vagrant tempests, and the bare wood beneath had been cracked by scores of winters and bleached by as many summers' suns.

Elizabeth Akeley looked once at the ramshackle structure, nodded to herself and set out slowly to walk to it. Vernon

Whiteside placed himself at her elbow and Ezra Noyes set a pace a short stride behind the others, but Akeley halted at once, turned and gestured silently but decisively to them both to remain behind. She then resumed her progress through the copse.

Whiteside watched Elizabeth Akeley proceeding slowly but with apparently complete self-possession through the wooded area. She halted just outside the shack, leaned forward and slightly to one side as if peering through a cobwebbed window frame, then proceeded again. She tugged at the door, managed to drag it open with a squeal of rusted metal and protesting wood and disappeared inside the shack.

'Are you just going to let her go like that?' Ezra Noyes demanded of Whiteside. 'How do you know who's in there? What if it's a Beta Reticulan? What if it's a Moth Man? What if there's a whole bunch of aliens in there? They might have a tunnel from the shack to their saucer. The whole thing might be a front. Shouldn't we go after her?'

Whiteside shook his head. 'Mother Akeley issued clear instructions, Ezra. We are to wait here.' He reached inside his jacket and unobtrusively flicked on the concealed microcassette recorder. When he pulled his hand from his pocket he brought with it the earphone. He adjusted it carefully in his ear.

'Oh, I didn't know you were deaf,' Noyes said.

'Just a little,' Whiteside replied.

'Well, what are we going to do?' Ezra asked him.

'I shall wait for the Radiant Mother,' Whiteside told him. 'There is nothing to fear. Have faith in the Spiritual Light, little brother, and your footsteps will be illuminated.'

'Oh.' Ezra made a sour face and climbed onto the roof of Ambassador. He seated himself there, cross-legged, to watch for any evidence of activity at the shack.

Vernon Whiteside also kept watch on the shack, but chiefly he was listening to the voices transmitted by the cordless microphone concealed behind Elizabeth

Akeley's lapel. Excerpts from the transcript later made of these transmissions follow;

Microcassette, August 8, 1979
Voice #5 (Elizabeth Akeley): Hello? Hello? Is there —
Voice #6 (Unidentified voice; oddly metallic intonation; accent similar to male New England twang present in San Diego trance tapes): Come in, come in, don't be afraid.
Voice #5: It's so dark in here.
Voice #6: I'm sorry. Move carefully. You are perfectly safe but there is some delicate apparatus set up.
(Sounds of movement, feet shuffling, breathing, a certain vague *buzzing* sound. Creak as of a person sitting in an old wooden rocking chair.)
Voice #5: I can hardly see. Where are you?
Voice #6: The cells are very sensitive. My friends are not here. You are not Albert Wilmarth.
Voice #5: No, I don't even —
Voice #6: (Interrupting) Oh, my God!

158

Of course not. It's been so — tell me, what year is this?

Voice #5: 1979.

Voice #6: Poor Albert. Poor Albert. He could have come along. But of course he — what did you say your name was, young woman?

Voice #5: Akeley. Elizabeth Akeley.

(Silence. Buzzing sound. A certain unsettling sound as of wings rustling, but wings larger than those of any creature known to be native to Vermont.)

Voice #6: Do not taunt me, young woman!

Voice #5: Taunt you? Taunt you?

Voice #6: Do you know who I *am*? Does the name Henry Wentworth Akeley mean nothing to you?

(Pause . . . buzzing . . . rustling.)

Voice #5: Yes! Yes! Oh, oh, this is incredible! This is wonderful! It means — Yes, my grandfather spoke of you. If you're really — My grandfather was George Akeley. He — we —

Voice #6: (Interrupting) Then I am your great-grandfather, Miss Akeley. I regret that I cannot offer you my hand.

George Akeley was my son. Tell me, is he still alive?

Voice #5: No, he — he died. He died in 1971, eight years ago. I was a little girl, but I remember him speaking of his father in Vermont. He said you disappeared mysteriously. But he always expected to hear from you again. He even founded a church. The Spiritual Light Brotherhood. He never lost faith. I have continued his work. Waiting for word from — beyond. That's why I came when I — when I started receiving messages.

Voice #6: Thank you. Thank you, Elizabeth. Perhaps I should not have stayed away so long, but the vistas, my child, the vistas! How old did you say you were?

Voice #5: Why — why — eighteen. Almost nineteen.

(Buzzing.)

Voice #6: You have followed my directions, Elizabeth? You are alone? Yes? Good. The cells are very sensitive. I can see you, even in this darkness, even if you cannot see me. Elizabeth, I have been gone from Earth for half a century, yet I am no older than the day I — departed — in the year 1928. The sights I have seen, the dimensions and the galaxies I have visited! Not alone, my child. Of course not alone. Those ones who took me — ah, child! Human flesh is too weak, too fragile to travel beyond the earth.

Voice #5: But there are spacesuits. Rockets. Capsules. Oh, I suppose that was after your time. But we've visited the moon. We've sent instruments to Venus and Mars and the moons of Jupiter.

Voice #6: And what you know is what Columbus might have learned of the New World, by paddling a rowboat around the port of Cadiz! Those ones who took me, those Old Ones! They can fly between the worlds on their great ribbed wings! They can span the very aether of space as a dragonfly flits across the surface of a pond! They are the greatest scientists, the greatest naturalists, the greatest anthropologists, the greatest explorers in the universe! Those whom they select to accompany them, if they cannot survive the ultimate vacuum of space, the Old Ones discard their bodies and seal their brains in metal canisters and carry them from world to world, from star to burning, glittering star!

(Buzzing, loud sound of rustling.)

Voice #5: Then — you have been to other worlds? Other planets, other physical worlds. Not other planes of spiritual existence. Our congregants believe —

Voice #6: (Interrupting) Your congregants doubtlessly believe poppycock. Yes, I have been to other worlds. I have seen all the planets of the solar system, from little, sterile Mercury to giant, distant Yuggoth.

Voice #5: Distant Yu — Yuggoth?

Voice #6: Yes, yes. I suppose those fool astronomers have yet to find it, but it is the gem and the glory of the solar system, glowing with its own ruby-red glare. It revolves in its own orbit, turned ninety degrees from the plane of the ecliptic. No wonder they've never seen it. They don't know where to look. Yet it perturbs the paths of Neptune and Pluto. That ought to be clue enough! Yuggoth is very nearly a sun. It possesses its own corps of worldlets, Nithon, Zaman, the miniature twins Thog and Thok! And there is life there! There is the Ghooric Zone where bloated shoggoths splash and spawn!

Voice #5: I can't — I can't believe all this! My own great-grandpa! Planets and beasts . . .

Voice #6: Yuggoth was merely the beginning for me. Those Ones carried me far away from the sun. I have seen the worlds that circle Arcturus and Centaurus, Wolf and Barnard's Star and Beta Reticuli. I have seen creatures whose physical embodiment would send a sane man mad into screaming nightmares of horror that never end and whose minds and souls would put to shame the proudest achievements of Einstein and Schopenhauer, Confucius and Plato, the Enlightened One and the Anointed One! And I have known love, child, love such as no earthbound mortal has ever known.

Voice #5: Lo — love, Great-Grandfather?

(Sound of buzzing, loud and agitated rustling of wings.)

Voice #6: You know about love, surely, Elizabeth. Doesn't your church preach a gospel of love? In fifty-seven years on this planet I never came across a church that didn't claim that. And have you known love? A girl your age, surely you've known the feeling by now.

Voice #5: Yes, Great-Grandfather.

Voice #6: Is it merely a physical attraction, Elizabeth? Do you believe that souls can love? Or do you believe in such things as souls? Can *minds* love one another?

Voice #5: All three. All three of those.

Voice #6: Good. Yes, all three. And when two beings love with their minds and their souls, they yearn also for bodies with which to express their love. Hence the physical manifestation of love. (Pause.) Excuse me, child. In a way I suppose I'm nothing but an old man rambling on about abstractions. You have a young man, have you?

Voice #5: Yes.

Voice #6: I would like to meet him. I would like very much to meet him, my child.

Voice #5: Great-Grandfather. May I tell the people about you?

Voice #6: No, Elizabeth. The time is not ripe.

Voice #5: But this is the most important event since — since — (Pause.) Contact with other beings, with other races, not of the earth. Proof that there is intelligent life throughout the universe. Proof of visits between the worlds and between the galaxies.

Voice #6: All in time, child. Now I am tired. Please go now. Will you visit me again?

Voice #5: Of course. Of course.

★   ★   ★

Elizabeth Akeley emerged from the shack, took one step and staggered.

At the far side of the copse of trees, Vernon Whiteside and Ezra Noyes watched. They saw Elizabeth. Ezra scrambled from the roof of the station wagon. Whiteside started forward, prepared to assist Mother Akeley.

But she had merely been blinded, for the moment, by the bright sunlight of a Vermont August. Whiteside and Ezra

Noyes saw her returning through the glade. Once or twice she stopped and leaned against a strangely spongy tree. Each time she started again, to all appearances further debilitated rather than restored.

She reached the station wagon and leaned against its drab metalwork. Whiteside said, 'Are you all right, Radiant Mother?'

She managed a wan smile. 'Thank you, Vernon. Yes, I'm all right. Thank you.'

Ezra Noyes was beside himself.

'Who was in there? What was going on? Were there really aliens in that shack? Can I go? Oh, darn it, darn it!' He pounded one fist into the palm of his other hand. 'I should never have left home without my camera! Kenneth Arnold himself said that back in '47. It's the prime directive of all Ufologists and I went off without one, me of all people. Oh, darn, darn, darn!'

Vernon Whiteside said, 'Radiant Mother, do you wish to leave now? May I visit the shack first?'

'Please, Vernon, don't. I asked him'

— She drew Whiteside away from Noyes — 'I asked him if I could reveal this to the world and he said, not yet.'

'I monitored the tape, Reverend Mother.'

'Yes.'

'What does it mean, Reverend Mother?'

She passed her hand across her face, tugging soft bangs across her eyes to block out the bright sunlight. 'I feel faint, Vernon. Ask Ezra to drive us back to Dark Mountain, would you?'

He helped her climb into the station wagon and signaled to Ezra. 'Mother Akeley is fatigued. She must be taken back at once.'

Ezra sighed and started the Ambassador's straight-six engine.

Elizabeth Akeley telephoned Marc Feinman from the Noyes house in Dark Mountain. A message had been transmitted surreptitiously by Agent Whiteside in time for monitoring arrangements to be made. Neither Akeley nor Feinman was aware of the monitoring system.

Excerpts from the call follow:

August 9, 1979 (outgoing)

Voice #2 (Sara Feinman): Yes.

Voice #5 (Elizabeth Akeley): Mrs. Feinman?

Voice #2: Yes, who is this?

Voice #5: Mrs. Feinman, this is Elizabeth Akeley speaking. I'm a friend of Marc's from San Diego. Is Marc there, please?

Voice #2: I know all about Marc's friend, Elizabeth darling. Don't you know Marc's father is in the hospital? Should you be bothering Marc at such a time?

Voice #5: I'm very sorry about Mr. Feinman, Mrs. Feinman. Marc told me before he left California. Is he all right?

Voice #2: Don't ask.

(Pause.)

Voice #5: Could I speak with Marc? Please?

Voice #2: (Off-line, pick-up is very faint) Marc, here, it's your little goyishe priestess. Yes. On the telephone. No, she didn't say where. No, she didn't say.

Voice #1 (Marc Feinman): Lizzy? Lizzy baby, are you okay?

168

Voice #5: Yes, I'm okay. Is your father —

Voice #1: (Interrupting) They operated this morning. I saw him after. He's very weak, Liz. But I think he's going to make it. Lizzy, where are you? Pleasant Street?

Voice #5: Vermont.

Voice #1: What? *Vermont?*

Voice #5: I couldn't wait, Marc. You were on the road, and there was another trance. I couldn't wait till you arrived in New York. Vernon came with me. We're staying with a family in Dark Mountain. Marc, I met my great-grandfather. Yesterday. I tried to call you last night but —

Voice #1: I was at the hospital with Ma, visiting my father. We couldn't just —

Voice #5: Of course, Marc. You did the right thing. (Pause) How soon can you get here?

Voice #1: I can't leave now. My father is still — they're not sure. (Lowering voice.) I don't want to talk too loud. The doctor said it's going to be touch and go for at least forty-eight hours. I can't leave Ma.

Voice #5: (Sobs.) I understand, Marc.

But — but — my great-grandfather . . .

Voice #1: How old is the old coot? He must be at least ninety.

Voice #5: He was born in 1871. He's one hundred and eight.

Voice #1: My God! Talk about tough old Yankee stock!

Voice #5: It isn't that, Marc! It has to do with the trance messages. Don't you understand? All of that strange material about alien beings, and other galaxies? That was no sci-fi trip —

Voice #1: I never said you were making it up, Lizzy! Your subconscious, though, I mean, you see some TV show or a movie and —

Voice #5: But that's just it, Marc! Those are real messages. Not from my subconscious. My great-grandpa was sending, oh, call them spirit messages or telepathic radiations or anything you like. He's here. He's back. Aliens took him away, they took his brain in a metal cylinder and he's been travelling in outer space for fifty years and now he's back here in Vermont and —

Voice #1: Okay, Lizzy, enough! Look,

I'll drive up there as soon as I can get away. As soon as my father's out of danger. I can't leave my ma now but as soon as I can. What's this place . . . ?

★   ★   ★

Late on the afternoon of August 9, Ezra Noyes rapped on the door of Elizabeth Akeley's room. She admitted him and he stood in the center of the room, nervously wondering whether it would be proper to sit in her presence. Akeley urged him to sit. The conversation which ensued was recalled by young Noyes in a deposition taken later at an Agency field office. Excerpts from the deposition follow:

'Well, you see, I told her that I was really serious about UFOs and all that stuff. She didn't know much about Ufology. She'd never heard about the men in black, even, so I told her all about them so she'd be on the lookout. I asked her who this Vernon Whiteside was, and she said he was the sexton of her church and completely reliable and I shouldn't worry about him.

'I showed her some copies of the *Intelligencer* and she said she liked the mag a lot and asked if she could keep them. I said sure. Anyway, she wanted to know how long the Moth Man sightings had been going on. I told her, only about six months ago over at Townshend or around here. Then she asked me what I knew about a rash of similar sightings about fifty years ago.

'That was right up my alley. You know, I did a lot of research. I went down and read a lot of old newspaper files. They have the old papers on microfilm now, it kills your eyes to crouch over a reader all day looking at the old stuff, but it's really interesting.

'Anyway, there were some odd sightings back in the '20s, and then when they had those floods around here in November of '27, there were some really strange things. They found some bodies, parts of bodies that is, carried downstream in the flood. There were some in the Winooski River over near Montpelier, and some right in the streets of Passumpsic. The town was flooded, you know.

'Strange bodies. Things like big wings. Not like moth wings, though. More like bat wings. And there seems to have been some odd goings on with Miss Akeley's great-grandfather, Henry Akeley. He was a retired prof, you know. And something about a friend of his, a guy called Al Wilmarth. But it was all hushed up.

'Well, I told Miss Akeley everything I knew and then I asked her who was in the cabin over at that dirt road near Lyndonville. I think she must have got mixed up, because she said it was Henry Akeley. He disappeared in 1927 or '28. Even if he turned up, he couldn't be alive by now. She said he said something to her about love, and about wanting a young man's body and a young woman's body so he could make love with some woman from outer space, he said from Aldebaran. I guess you have to be a sci-fi nut to know about Aldebaran. I'm a sci-fi nut. I don't say too much about it in UFO circles — they don't like sci-fi, they think the sci-fi crowd put down UFOs. They're scared of 'em. They want to keep it all nice and safe and imaginary, you ought to read Sanderson and Earley on that some time.

'Well, how could a human and an alien make love? I guess old Akeley must have thought something like mind-transfer, like one partner could take over the body of a member of the other partner's species, you know. Only be careful, don't try it with those spiders where the female eats the male after they mate. Ha-ha-ha! Ha-ha!

'But Miss Akeley kept asking about lovemaking, you know, and I started to wonder if maybe she wasn't hinting at something, you know. I mean, there we were in this room. And it was my own parents' house and all, but it *was* a bedroom, and I didn't want her to think that she could just walk in there and, uh, well, you know.

'So I excused myself then. But she seemed upset. She kept running her hand through her hair. Pulling it down, those strips, what do women call them, bangs, over her forehead. I told her I had to get to work on the next ish of my mag, you know, and she'd have to excuse me but the last ish had been late and I was trying to get the mag back on schedule. But I told her, if she wanted a lift over to Passumpsic again, I'd be glad to give her a ride over there any time, and I'd like to meet her great-grandfather if he was living in that old shack. Then she said he wasn't exactly living in the shack, but he sort of was, sort of was there and sort of was living there. It didn't make any sense to me, so I went and started laying out the next issue of the *Intelligencer* 'cause I wanted to get it out on time for once, and show those guys that I can get a mag out on time when I get a chance.

'Anyway, Miss Akeley said her great-grandfather's girl-friend was named something like Sheera from Aldebaran. I told her that sounded like something out of a bad '50s sci-fi flick on the TV. There's a great channel in Montreal, we get it on the cable, they show sci-fi flicks every week. And that sure sounded like a sci-fi flick to me.

'Sheera from Aldebaran! Ha-ha-ha! Ha-ha!'

Marc Feinman wheeled his Ferrari up to the Noyes home. His sporty driving-cap was cocked over one ear. Suede jacket, silk shirt, Gucci jeans and Frye boots completed his outfit.

The front door swung in as Fienman's boot struck the bottom wooden step. Elizabeth Akeley was across the white-washed porch and in Feinman's arms before he reached the top of the flight. Without releasing his embrace of Akeley, Feinman extended one hand to grasp that of Vernon Whiteside.

They entered the house. Ezra Noyes greeted them in the front parlor. Elizabeth and Vernon briefed Marc on the events since their arrival in Vermont. When the narrative was brought up to date, Feinman asked simply, 'What do you want to do?'

Ezra started to blurt out an ambitious plan for gaining the confidence of the aliens and arranging a ride in their saucer, but Whiteside, still maintaining the role of sexton of the Spiritual Light

Church, cut him off. 'We will do whatever the Radiant Mother asks us to do.'

All eyes turned to Akeley.

After an uncomfortable interval she said, 'I was — hoping that Marc could help. It's so strange, Marc. I know that I'm the one who always believed in — in the spirit world. The beyond. What you always call the supernormal.'

Feinman nodded.

'But somehow,' Elizabeth went on, 'this seems more like your ideas than mine. It's so — I mean, this is the kind of thing that I've always looked for, believed in. And you haven't. And now that it's true, it doesn't seem to have any spiritual meaning. It's just — something that you could explain with your logic and your computers.'

Feinman rubbed his slightly blue chin with his free hand. 'This great-grandpa of yours, this Henry Akeley . . . '

He looked into her eyes.

'You say, he was talking about some kind of mating ritual?'

Liz nodded.

Feinman said, 'What did he look like?

Did you ever see your great-grandfather before? Even a picture? Maybe one that your grandfather had in San Diego?'

She shook her head. 'No. At least, I don't remember ever seeing a photo at home. There might have been one. But I hardly saw anything in the shack, Marc.'

Ezra Noyes was jumping up and down in his chair. 'Yes, you never told us, Lizzy — Miss Akeley. What did you see? What did he look like?'

'I hardly saw anything!' Liz covered her face with her hands, dropped one to her lap, tugged nervously at her bangs with the other. 'It was pitch dark in there. Just a little faint light seeping between the cracks in the walls, through those broken windows. The windows that weren't broken were so filthy they wouldn't let any light in.'

'So you couldn't tell if it was really Henry Akeley.'

'It was the same voice,' Vernon Whiteside volunteered. 'We, ah, we bugged the meeting, Mr. Feinman. The voice was the same as the one on the trance tapes from the church.'

Feinman's eyes widened. 'The same? But the trance tapes are in Lizzy's voice!'

Whiteside back-pedaled. 'No, you're right. I don't suppose they were the same vocal chords. But the timbre. And the enunciation. Everything. Same person speaking. I'd stake my reputation on it!'

Feinman stroked his chin again. 'All right. Here's what I'd like to do. Lizzy, Henry Akeley said he'd see you again, right? Okay, let's surprise him. Suppose Whiteside and I head out there. Can you find the shack again, Vernon? Good! Okay, we'll take the Ferrari out there.'

'But it's nearly dark out.'

'No difference if it's so damned dark inside the shack! I've got a good five-cell torch in the emergency kit in the Ferrari.'

'I ought to come along,' Ezra Noyes put in. 'I *do* represent the Vermont UFO Intelligence Bureau, you know!'

'Right,' Feinman nodded. 'And we'll need your help later. No, we'll need you, Ezra, but not right now. Whiteside and I will visit Henry Akeley — or whoever or whatever is out there claiming to be Henry Akeley. Give us a couple of hours' head start. And then, you come ahead.'

'Can I get into the shack this time?' Ezra jumped up and paced nervously, almost danced, back and forth. 'The other time, I had to wait at the car. If I can get into the shack, I can get some photos. I'll rig up a flash on my Instamatic. I want to get some shots of the inside of that cabin for the *Intelligencer*.'

'Yes, sure.' Feinman turned from Ezra Noyes and took Elizabeth Akeley's hand. 'You don't mind, do you, Lizzy? I'm worried that your ancestor there — or whoever it is — has some kind of control over you. Those trances — what if he puts you under some kind of hypnotic influence while we're all out there together?'

'How do you know he's evil? You seem to — just assume that Henry Akeley wants to harm me.'

'I don't know that at all.' Feinman frowned. 'I just have a nasty feeling about it. I want to get there first. I think Whiteside and I can handle things, and then you can arrive in a while. Please, Lizzy. You did call me to help. You didn't have to, you could just have gone back and never said anything to me until it was over.'

Elizabeth looked very worried. 'Maybe I should have.'

'Well, but you didn't. Now, can we do it my way? Please?'

'All right, Marc.'

Feinman turned to Vernon Whiteside. 'Let's go. How long a ride is it out there?'

Whiteside paused. 'Little less than an hour.'

Feinman grunted. 'Okay. Vernon and I will start now. We'll need about another hour once we're there, I suppose — call it two to be on the safe side. Lizzy and Ezra, if you'll follow us out to the shack in two hours, just come ahead in, we'll be there.'

Ezra departed to check his camera. Vernon accompanied Marc. Shortly the Ferrari Boxer disappeared in a cloud of yellow Vermont dust, headed for Passumpsic.

As soon as they had pulled out of sight of the house, Vernon spoke. 'Mr. Feinman, I've been helping Radiant Mother on this trip.'

'I know that, Vernon. Lizzy mentioned it several times. I really appreciate it.'

'Mr. Feinman, you know how concerned Radiant Mother is about Church archives. The way she records her sermons and the message services. Well, she was worried about her meeting with old Mr. Akeley. So I helped her to rig a wireless mike on her jacket, so we got a microcassette of the meeting.'

Feinman said he knew that.

'Well, if you don't mind, I'd like to do the same again.' Whiteside held the tiny microcassette recorder for Feinman to see. The Ferrari's V-12 purred throatily, loafing along the Passumpsic road in third gear.

'Sure. That's a good idea. But you needn't rig me up. I want you along. You can just mike yourself.'

Vernon Whiteside considered. 'Tell you what . . . ' He reached into his pocket, pulled out a pair of enamel ladybugs. 'I'll mike us both. If we happen to pick up the same sounds there'll be no harm. In fact, it'll give us a redundancy check. If we get separated — '

'I don't see why we should.'

'Just in case.' He pinned a ladybug to Feinman's suede jacket, attached the second bug to his own. He made a minor adjustment to the recorder.

'There.' He slipped the recorder back into his pocket. 'I separated the input circuits. Now we'll record on two channels. We can mix the sound if we record the same events or keep it separate if we pick up different events. In fact, just to be on the safe side, suppose I leave the recorder here in the car when you and I go to the shack.'

Feinman assented and Whiteside peeled the sealers from a dime-sized disk of double-adhesive foam. He stuck it to the recorder and stuck the recorder to the bottom of the Ferrari's dashboard.

'For the sexton of the Spiritual Light Church,' Feinman said, 'you know a hell of a lot about electronics.'

'My sister's boy, Mr. Feinman. Bright youngster. It's his hobby. Started out with a broken Victrola. Got his science teacher to helping. Going to San Diego State next term. I couldn't be prouder if he was my own boy. He builds all sorts of gadgets.'

Feinman tooled the Ferrari around the dome-topped hill and pulled to a halt where the Noyes station wagon had parked on the earlier visit. The sun was setting and the somehow too-lush glade was filled with murk.

Vernon Whiteside reached under the dashboard and flicked the microcassette recorder to automatic mode. He climbed from the car.

Feinman went to the rear of the Ferrari and extracted a long-handled electric torch. He pulled his sports cap down over his eyes and touched Whiteside's elbow. The men advanced.

The events that transpired following this entrance to the sycamore copse were captured on the microcassette recorder, and a transcript of these sounds appears later in the report.

In the meanwhile, Elizabeth Akeley and Ezra Noyes waited at the Noyes home in Dark Mountain.

Two hours to the minute after the departure of Marc Feinman and Vernon Whiteside in Feinman's Ferrari Boxer, the Noyes station wagon, its aged suspension creaking, pulled out of the driveway.

Ezra pushed the Nash to the limit of its tired ability, chattering the while to Elizabeth. Preoccupied, she responded with low monosyllables. At the turning-point from the Passumpsic — Lyndonville road onto the old farm track, she waited in the station wagon while Ezra climbed down and opened the fence gate.

The Nash's headlights picked a narrow path for the car, circling the dome-topped hill that blocked the copse of lush vegetation from the sight of passers-by. The Ferrari Boxer stood silently at the edge of the copse.

Ezra lifted his camera-bag from the floor and slung it over his shoulder. Elizabeth waited in the car until Ezra walked to her side, opened the door and offered his hand.

They started through the copse. Noyes testified later that this was his first experience with the unusual vegetation. He claimed that, even as he set foot beneath the overhanging branches of the first sycamore a strange sensation passed through him. The day had been hot and even in the hours of darkness the temperature did not drop drastically. Even so, with his entry into the copse Noyes felt an unnatural and debilitating heat, as if the trees were adapted to a different climate than that of northern Vermont and were actually emitting heat of their own.

He began to perspire.

Elizabeth Akeley led the way through the wooded area, retracing the steps of her previous visit to the wooden shack.

Noyes found it more and more difficult to continue. With each pace he felt drained of energy and will. Once he halted and was about to sit down for a rest but Akeley grasped his hand and pulled him along.

When they emerged from the copse the dome-topped hill stood directly behind them, the rundown shack directly ahead.

Ezra and Elizabeth crossed the narrow grassy patch between the sycamore copse and the ramshackle cabin. Ezra found a space where the glass had fallen away and there was a small opening in the omnipresent cobwebs. He peered in, then lifted his camera and poked its lens through the opening. He shot a picture.

'Don't know what I got, but maybe I got something,' he said.

Elizabeth Akeley pulled the door open. She stepped inside the cabin, closely followed by young Noyes.

The room, Ezra could see, was far larger than he'd estimated. Although the shack contained but a single room, that was astonishingly deep, its far corners utterly lost in shadow. Near to him were a rocking chair, a battered overstuffed couch and a dust-laden wooden table of a type often found in old New England homes.

Ezra later reported hearing odd sounds during these minutes. There was a strange buzzing sound. He couldn't tell whether it was organic — a sound such as a flight of hornets might have made, or such as might have been made by a single insect magnified to a shocking gigantism — or whether the sound was artificial, as if an electrical generator were running slightly out of adjustment.

The modulation was its oddest characteristic. Not only did the volume rise and fall, but the pitch, and in some odd way, the very tonal quality of the buzzing, kept changing. 'It was as if something was trying to talk to me. To us. To Miss Akeley and me. I could almost understand it, but not quite.'

Noyes stood, paralyzed, until he heard Elizabeth Akeley scream. Then he whirled, turning his back to the table from whence the buzzing sounds were coming. He saw Elizabeth standing before the rocking chair, her hands to her face.

The chair was rocking slowly, gently. The cabin was almost pitch black, its only illumination coming from an array of unfamiliar machinery set up on the long wooden table. Ezra could see now that a figure was seated, apparently unmoving, in the rocker.

It spoke.

'Elizabeth, my darling, you have come,' the figure said. 'Now we shall be together. We shall know the love of the body as we have known the love of the mind and of the soul.'

Strangely, Noyes later stated, although the voice in which the figure spoke was that of Marc Feinman, the accent and intonation were those of a typical New England old-timer. Noyes testified also that his powers of observation played a strange trick on him at this moment. Although the man sitting in the chair was undoubtedly Marc Feinman — the clothing he wore, even to the sporting cap pulled low over his eyes, as if he were driving his Ferrari in bright sunlight — what Ezra noticed most particularly was a tiny red-and-black smudge on Feinman's jacket.

'It looked like a squashed lady bug,' the youth stated later.

From somewhere in the darker corners of the cabin there came a strange rustling sound, like that of great leathery wings opening and folding again.

Noyes shot a quick series of pictures, one of the figure in the rocking chair, one of the table with the unusual mechanical equipment on it, and one of the darker corners of the cabin, hoping vaguely that he would get some results. The rocking chair tilted slowly backward, slowly forward. The man sitting in it finally said to Ezra, 'You'll never get anything from there. You'd better get over to the other end of the shack and make your pictures.'

As if hypnotized, Noyes walked toward the rear of the cabin. He stated later that as he passed a certain point, it was as if he had penetrated a curtain of total darkness. He tried to turn and look back at the others, but could not move. He tried to call out but could not speak. He was completely conscious, but seemingly had plunged into a state of total paralysis and of sensory deprivation.

What transpired behind him, in the front end of the cabin, he could not tell. When he recovered from his paralysis and loss of sensory inputs, it was to find himself alone at the rear of the shack. It was daylight outside and sunshine was pushing through the grimy windows and open door of the shanty. He turned around and found himself facing two figures. A third was at his side.

'Ezra!' The third figure said.

'Mr. Whiteside.' Noyes responded.

'Well, I'm glad to see that you two are all right,' a voice came to them from the other end of the cabin. It was the old New England twang that Ezra had heard from the man in the rocking chair, and the speaker was, indeed, Marc Feinman. He stood, wooden-faced, his back to the doorway. Elizabeth Akeley, her features similarly expressionless, stood at his side. Feinman's sporting cap was pulled down almost to the line of his eyebrows. Akeley's bangs dangled over her forehead.

Noyes claimed later that he thought he could see signs of a fresh red scar running across Akeley's forehead beneath the bangs. He claimed also that a corner of red was visible at the edge of the visor of Feinman's cap. But of course this is unverified.

'We're going now,' Feinman said in his strange New England twang. 'We'll take my car. You two go home in the other.'

'But — but, Radiant Mother,' Whiteside began.

'Elizabeth is very tired,' Feinman said

nasally. 'You'll have to excuse her. I'm taking her away for a while.'

He started out the door, guiding Elizabeth by the elbow. She walked strangely, yet not as if she were tired, ill, or even injured. Rather, she had the tentative, uncertain movements that are associated with an amputee first learning to maneuver on prosthetic devices.

They left the cabin and walked to the Ferrari. Feinman opened the door on the passenger side and guided Akeley into the car. Then he circled the vehicle, climbed in and seated himself at the wheel. Strangely, he sat for a long time staring at the controls of the sports car, as if he were unfamiliar with its type.

Vernon Whiteside and Ezra Noyes followed the others from the cabin. Both were still confused from their strange experience of paralysis and sensory deprivation; both stated later that they felt only half-awake, half-hypnotized. 'Else,' Agent Whiteside later deposed, 'I'd have stopped 'em for sure. Warrant or no warrant, I had probable cause that something fishy was going on, and I'd have grabbed the keys out of that Ferrari, done anything it took to keep those two there. But I could hardly move, I could hardly even think.

'I *did* manage to reach into that car and grab out my machine. My microcassette recorder. Then I looked at my little bug-mike and saw that it was squashed, like somebody'd just squeezed it between his thumb and his finger, only he must have been made out of iron 'cause those bug-mikes are ruggedized. They can take a wallop with a sledgehammer and not even know it. So who squashed my little bug?

'Then Feinman finally got his car started and they pulled away. I looked at the Noyes kid and he looked at me, and we headed for his Nash wagon and we went back to his house. Nearly cracked up half a dozen times on the way home, he drove like a drunk. When we got to his place we both passed out for twelve hours while Feinman and Akeley were going God-knows-where in that Ferrari.

'Soon as I got myself back together I

phoned in to Agency field HQ and came on in.'

When Agent Whiteside reported to Agency field HQ he turned over the microcassette which he and Feinman had made at the shack. Excerpts from the tape follow.

(Whiteside's Channel)

(All voices mixed): Yeah, this is the place all right . . . I'll — got it open, okay . . . Sheesh, it's dark in here. How'd she see anything? Well . . . (Buzzing sound.) What's that? What's that? Here, I'll shine my — what the hell? It looks like . . . Shining cylinder. No, two of 'em. Two of 'em. What the hell, some kind of futuristic espresso machines. What the hell . . .

(Buzzing sound becomes very loud, dominates tape. Then volume drops and a rustling is heard.)

Voice #3 (Vernon Whiteside): Here, lend me that thing a minute. No, I just gotta see what's over there. Okay, you stay here a minute, I gotta see what's . . .

(Sound of walking. Buzzing continues

in background but fades, rustling sound increases.)

Voice #3: Jesus God! That can't be! No, no, that can't be! It's too . . .

(Sound of thump, as if microphone were being struck and then crushed between superhard metallic surfaces. Remainder of Whiteside channel is silent.)

(Feinman Channel)

(Early portion identical to Whiteside channel; excerpts begin following end of recording on Whiteside channel.)

Voice #1 (Marc Feinman): Vernon? Vernon? What —

Voice #6 (Henry Wentworth Akeley): He is unharmed.

Voice #1: Who's that?

Voice #6: I am Henry Wentworth Akeley.

Voice #1: Lizzy's great-grandfather.

Voice #6: Precisely. And you are Mr. Feinman?

Voice #1: Where are you, Akeley?

Voice #6: I am here.

Voice #1: Where? I don't see . . . what happened to Whiteside? What's going on here? I don't like what's going on here.

Voice #6: Please, Mr. Feinman, try to remain calm.

Voice #1: Where are you, Akeley? For the last time . . .

Voice #6: Please, Mr. Feinman, I must ask you to calm yourself. (Rustling sound.) Ah, that's better. Mr. Feinman, do you not see certain objects on the table? Good. Now, Mr. Feinman, you are an intelligent and courageous young man. I understand that your interests are wide and your thirst for knowledge great. I offer you a grand opportunity. One which was offered to me half a century ago. I tried to decline at that time. My hand was forced. I never regretted having . . . let us say, gone where I have gone. But I must now return to earthly flesh, and as my own integument is long destroyed, I have need of another.

Voice #1: What — where — what are you talking about? If this is some kind of . . .

(Loud sound of rustling, sound of thumping and struggle, incoherent gasps and gurgles, loud breathing, moans.)

(At this point the same sound that ended the Whiteside segment of the tape is heard. Remainder of Feinman channel is blank.)

★ ★ ★

When Agent Whiteside and young Ezra Noyes woke from their exhausted sleep, Whiteside identified himself as a representative of the Agency. He obtained the film from young Noyes's camera. It was promptly developed at the nearest Agency facility. The film was subsequently returned to Noyes and the four usable photographs, in fuzzily screened and mimeographed form, appeared in the *Vermont UFO Intelligencer*.

A description of the four photographs follows:

Frame 1: (Shot through window of the wooden shack) A dingy room containing a rocking chair and a large wooden table.

Frame 2: (Shot inside room) A rocking chair. In the chair is sitting a man identified as Marc Feinman. Feinman's sporting cap is pulled down covering his forehead. His eyes are barely visible and seem to have a glazed appearance, but this may be due to the unusual lighting conditions. A mark on his forehead seems to be visible at the edge of the cap, but is insufficiently distinct for verification.

Frame 3: (Shot inside room) Large wooden table holding unusual mechanical apparatus. There are numerous electrical devices, power units, what appears to be a cooling unit, photoelectric cells, items which appear to be microphones, and two medium-sized metallic cylinders estimated to contain sufficient space for a human brain, along with compact life-support paraphernalia.

Frame 4: (Shot inside room) This was obviously Noyes's final frame, taken as he headed toward the darkened rear area of the cabin. The rough wooden flooring before the camera is clearly visible. From it there seems to rise a curtain or wall of sheer blackness. This is not a black *substance* of any sort, but a curtain or mass of sheer negation. All attempts at analysis by Agency photoanalysts have failed completely.

198

★ ★ ★

Elizabeth Akeley and Marc Feinman were located at — of all places — Niagara Falls, New York. They had booked a honeymoon cottage and were actually located by representatives of the Agency returning in traditional yellow slickers from a romantic cruise on the craft *Maid of the Mist*.

Asked to submit voluntarily to Agency interrogation, Feinman refused. Akeley, at Feinman's prompting, simply shook her head negatively. 'But I'll tell you what,' Feinman said in a marked New England twang, 'I'll make out a written statement for you if you'll settle for that.'

Representatives of the Agency considered this offer unsatisfactory, but having no grounds for holding Feinman or Akeley and being particularly sensitive to criticism of the Agency for alleged intrusion upon the religious freedoms of unorthodox cults, the representatives of the Agency were constrained to accept Feinman's offer.

The deposition provided by Feinman

— and co-sworn by Akeley — represented a vague and rambling narrative of no value. Its concluding paragraph follows:

*   *   *

All we want is to be left alone. We love each other. We're here now and we're happy here. What came before is over. That's somebody else's concern now. Let them go. Let them see. Let them learn. Vega, Aldebaran, Ophiuchi, the Crab Nebula. Let them see. Let them learn. Someday we may wish to go back. We will have a way to summon those Ones. When we summon those Ones they will respond.

*   *   *

A final effort by representatives of the Agency was made, in an additional visit to the abandoned shack by the sycamore copse off the Passumpsic — Lyndonville road. A squad of agents wearing regulation black outfits were guided by Vernon Whiteside. An additional agent remained at the Noyes home to assure non-interference by Ezra Noyes.

Whiteside guided his fellow agents to the sycamore copse. Several agents remarked at the warmth and debilitating feeling they experienced as they passed through the copse. In addition, an abnormal number of small cadavers — of squirrels, chipmunks, one grey fox, a skunk, and several whippoorwills — were noted, lying beneath the trees.

The shack contained an aged wooden rocking chair, a battered overstuffed couch, and a large wooden table. Whatever might have previously stood upon the table had been removed.

There was no evidence of the so-called wall or curtain of darkness. The rear of the shack was vacant.

★　★　★

In the months since the incidents above reported, two additional developments have taken place, note of which is appropriate herein.

First, Marc Feinman and Elizabeth

Akeley returned to San Diego in Feinman's Ferrari Boxer. There, they took up residence at the Pleasant Street location. Feinman vacated the Upas Street apartment; he returned to his work with the computer firm. Inquiries placed with his employers indicate that he appeared, upon returning, to be absent-minded and disoriented, and unexpectedly to require briefings in computer technology and programming concepts with which he had previously been thoroughly familiar.

Feinman explained this curious lapse by stating that he had experienced a head injury while vacationing in Vermont, and still suffered from occasional lapses of memory. He showed a vivid but rapidly fading scar on his forehead as evidence of the injury. His work performance quickly returned to its previous high standard. 'Marc's as smart as the brightest prof you ever studied under,' his supervisor stated to the Agency. 'But that Vermont trip made some impression on him! He picked up this funny New England twang in his speech, and it just won't go away.'

Elizabeth Akeley went into seclusion. Feinman announced that they had been married, and that Elizabeth was, at least temporarily, abandoning her position as Radiant Mother of the Spiritual Light Church, although remaining a faithful member of the Church. In Feinman's company she regularly attends Sunday worship services, but seldom speaks.

The second item of note is of questionable relevance and significance, but is included here as a matter of completing the appropriate documentation. Vermont Forestry Service officers have reported that a new variety of sycamore tree has appeared in the Windham County — Caledonia County section of the state. The new sycamores are lush and extremely hardy. They seem to generate a peculiarly *warm* atmosphere, and are not congenial to small forest animals. Forestry officers who have investigated report a strange sense of lassitude when standing beneath these trees, and one officer has apparently been lost while exploring a stand of the trees near the town of Passumpsic.

Brackish Waters

Delbert Marston, Jr., Ph.D., D.Sc., was the youngest tenured professor on the faculty of the University of California. He was widely regarded as a rising academic star, not only on the University's premiere campus at Berkeley but throughout the huge multi-campus system and, if the truth be known, throughout the national and international community of scholars.

Tall and dark-haired with a touch of premature grey at the temples, he was regarded as a catch by female faculty members who competed vigorously for his attention. He dressed conservatively, held his tongue in matters of both public and campus politics, drank single-malt scotch whiskey exclusively, and drove an onyx-black supercharged 1937 Cord Phaeton. Perhaps it was Marston's otherwise thoroughly conventional lifestyle that caused his vehicular preference to be regarded as a sign of high taste and acceptable self-indulgence rather than one of eccentricity.

He had the Cord serviced regularly at an exclusive garage on the island of Alameda, the owner of which establishment catered to fanciers of the three marques formerly built in Auburn, Indiana — the Auburn, the stately Duesenberg, and the tragically short-lived Cord. The Auburn Motor Car Company, or what was left of it, was now producing Lycoming aircraft engines and B-24 Liberator bombers for the Army Air Forces. Once the war was over there was no predicting the future of the discontinued automobiles but in Marston's estimation their prospects were poor.

On the night in question — the night, at any rate, that would initiate the series of events destined to lead to Delbert Marston's apotheosis — the sky above the San Francisco Bay Area was black with a cold storm that had swept down from the Gulf of Alaska and attacked the Pacific Coast with fierce winds and a series of hammering downpours of pelting rain laced with occasional hints of sleet. Such weather was not uncommon in Northern California during the winter months, and the winter of 1943–44 was no exception; the onslaught of wind and water was regarded as anything but freakish. The Bay Bridge was swept by an icy gale but the Cord held the roadway with a steadiness unmatched by vehicles of lesser quality.

Professor Marston was accompanied by an older colleague, one Aurelia Blenheim, Ph.D. Grey-haired and dignified, Professor Blenheim had served for some years as Marston's mentor and sponsor. It was her spirited championing of his cause that had persuaded the Tenure Committee to grant him its seal of approval despite what was regarded as his almost scandalous youth. Marston's intellectual equal, Aurelia Blenheim had found in the younger academic the friendship and platonic camaraderie that her lifelong celibacy had otherwise denied her.

'I don't know why I let you talk me into spending an evening with this squad of eccentrics, Aurelia.' Marston braked to keep his distance behind a superannuated Model A Ford that looked ready to topple over in the gale.

'Why, for the sheer pleasure and mental stimulation of bouncing off some people with unconventional ideas. Besides, the semester's over, most of the kiddies who have managed to stay out of the service have gone home to Bakersfield or Beloit or wherever they came from. What else did you have to do?'

'You've got to be kidding. The Oakland Symphony is doing an all-Mahler program, the San Francisco Ballet has a Berlioz show, and the opera is offering *The Marriage of Figaro*. And we're going to meet a bunch of wackos who think — if you can call it thinking . . . As a matter of fact, Aurelia, what in the world is it that they think?'

Aurelia Blenheim shook her head. 'Come now, Delbert. They have a lot of different ideas. That's the fun of it. They don't have a body of fixed beliefs. Attending one of their meetings is like sitting in on a First Century council of bishops and listening to them debate the

208

nature of the mystical body of Christ.'

'I can't think of anything less interesting.'

They had reached the San Francisco end of the bridge now and Marston maneuvered the Cord through merging traffic and headed south. A rattletrap Nash sedan full of high school kids pulled alongside the Cord. The driver lowered his window and yelled at Aurelia, 'Why don't you put that submarine back in the water where it belongs, grandma?'

Aurelia Blenheim turned to face the heckler and mouthed some words that remained unheard and unknown to Delbert Marston. The expression on the face of the heckler changed suddenly. He raised his window and floored his gas pedal. The Nash sped away. Three kids in the backseat stared open-mouthed at the grey-haired professor.

'Aurelia,' Marston asked, 'what did you say to them?'

'I just gave them a little warning, Delbert. Best keep your eyes on the road. I'll get us a little music.' She reached for the radio controls on the

Cord's dashboard. Although the radio had added to the price of Marston's Cord he had ordered it installed when he purchased the phaeton.

The sounds of Franz Liszt's *Mephisto Waltz* filled the Cord's tonneau.

A particularly dense sheet of rain mixed with a seeming bucketful of hailstones crashed against the Cord's roof and engine hood, adding the sound of an insane kettle drum concerto to the music.

'There's our exit sign,' Aurelia Blenheim shouted above the din.

Delbert Marston edged into the exit lane and guided the Cord off the highway and onto a local thoroughfare. Aurelia Blenheim navigated for him, giving instructions until she finally said: 'There it is. You can park in the driveway.'

The house stood out like an anomaly. Curwen Street and its environs — still known as Curwen Heights — had once been among San Francisco's more fashionable neighborhoods. Victorian homes had reared their turrets and cupolas against the chilly air and damply cloying fog. Families who claimed the status of municipal pioneers, direct descendants of the leaders of the Gold Rush and survivors of the earthquake and fire of 1906, had erected gingerbread-encrusted mansions and filled them with children and servants. Carriage-houses and stables were discreetly placed behind the family establishments.

But the passing decades had brought changes to Curwen Street and Curwen Heights. Urban crowding had driven the wealthiest families to Palo Alto, Burlingame and other lush, roomy suburbs. The construction of the Golden Gate Bridge and Bay Bridge in the 1930s had opened the unspoiled territories and sleepy villages of Marin and Alameda Counties for the use of daily commuters. Key Route trains brought workers from Oakland and Berkeley into the city each day.

Marston switched off the engine and half-blackened headlights, and climbed from behind the steering wheel. He exited the car and helped Aurelia Blenheim to do the same. He carefully locked the vehicle's doors and escorted her to the front entrance of the house. In the darkened street and with storm clouds blackening the sky it was difficult to see anything. Even so, the house had the appearance of a onetime showplace, long since fallen into disrepair. Blackout curtains made the windows look like shrouded paintings. Marston searched for a doorbell and found none. Instead, a heavy cast-iron knocker shaped like a gargoyle signaled their arrival.

The door swung open and they were greeted by a rotund individual wearing thick, horn-rimmed glasses. He peered owlishly at Marston, then dropped his gaze to Aurelia Blenheim.

'Dr. Blenheim!' He took her hand in both of his and pumped it enthusiastically. After he released her she introduced Marston. The rotund youth identified himself as Charlie Einstein ('No relation!'), subjected Marston's hand to the same treatment Aurelia Blenheim's had received, and ushered them into the house.

Voices were emerging from another

room, as was the odor of fried food. In the background a radio added to the din.

Charlie Einstein led Marston and Aurelia Blenheim to a high-ceilinged parlor. Men and women sat on worn furniture, each of them holding a plate of snack food or a beverage or both.

Einstein clapped his hands for attention and conversations wound down. The radio continued to play. Einstein said, 'Ben, would you mind?' He gestured toward a Philco console. 'You're the closest.'

A painfully thin and painfully young-looking man in a navy uniform reached for the Philco and switched it off. 'Nobody was paying attention anyhow,' he said. He turned toward Marston and Aurelia Blenheim. 'Aurelia, hello. And you must be Professor Marston.'

Del Marston nodded.

'Ben Keeler,' the sailor said. His spotless winter blues bore the eagle-and-chevron insignia of a petty officer. He shook Marston's hand. 'We've been hearing about you for weeks now, sir. I'm so pleased that you could finally make it to a meeting.'

Charlie Einstein set out to fetch beverages for Marston and Aurelia Blenheim. Keeler pointed out the others in the room, giving their names. Marston nodded to each.

One of them was a thirtyish woman whose mouse-brown sweater was a perfect match for her stringy hair. She was sitting next to the fireplace, where a log smoldered fitfully. 'This is Bernice,' Keeler announced. 'Bernice Sanderson.'

The woman looked up at Marston and Aurelia Blenheim. It was obvious that she knew Blenheim; they exchanged silent nods. 'So you're the famous professor.' She glared at Marston. 'The skeptic who doesn't believe in anything he can't see for himself. You've got a lot to learn, professor.'

She turned away.

Keeler took Marston by the elbow and steered him away. 'Sorry about that, sir.'

Marston interrupted. 'Please, just call me Del.'

'Fine.' The sailor grinned. 'You know, I was an undergrad at Cal until we got into this war. I'm accustomed to calling professors *sir*.' He reddened. 'Or, *ma'am*, Professor Bleinheim.'

'Aurie.'

'Yes.' Keeler turned a brighter shade of red. 'Anyway, once the war is over I plan to go back and finish up my degree.'

Marston nodded. He saw that Keeler wore an engineer's rating on his uniform sleeve. 'Good for you,' he said. 'There will be plenty of need for good engineers in the postwar world.'

Keeler said, 'Yes, sir. In fact — ' He was interrupted by Charlie Einstein carrying a tray with two steaming cups on it. 'I know Aurie likes these things and she told me that you did, too, Professor.'

'Del.'

'Right. Hot rum toddies. Good for a night like this.'

When Einstein went on his way, Ben Keeler resumed. 'I'd hoped to have you as my faculty adviser when I get to grad school. If I'm not being too pushy, that is.'

Marston shook his head. 'I'm flattered. Sure, come and see me when the war's over. I envy you, Ben, serving in the Navy.

You just went down and enlisted when Pearl Harbor was attacked?'

'I thought it was the right thing to do. In fact, I'd have thought that a man with your credentials would have a commission. If you don't mind my saying so, Professor. Del.'

Marston sipped at his rum toddy. 'They turned me down. Said I couldn't march right, and besides, they wanted me to hang around and lend my expertise when they had problems for me to play with. Said I was more valuable as a civilian than I would be in the Navy.'

Keeler nodded sympathetically.

Marston breathed a sigh of relief. The rum couldn't be that strong and fast-acting, it was just careless of him to mention not being able to march right. He'd been born with minor deformities of both feet. They'd never kept him from normal activities; in fact, he felt that they helped him as a swimmer. But the navy doctors had taken one look at his feet and told him to go home and find a way to contribute to the war effort as a civilian.

Still, the Navy had accepted him as a

consultant, calling upon his expertise as a marine geologist and hydrologist. He'd received a high security clearance and worked with naval personnel whenever he wasn't busy teaching. He looked around, observing that nearly everyone in the room was young. Aurelia Blenheim had persuaded Marston to attend a meeting, but this looked more like a party. There were plates of snack food scattered around the room and bottles of soft drinks. There was a low, steady hum of conversation. Marston spotted only two girls among the crowd, discounting the acerbic Miss Sanderson. Outnumbered as they were by males, they were twin centers of constant attention and maneuvering.

A fireplace dominated one end of the room. A young man of neurasthenic appearance wearing a baggy suit and hand-painted necktie had stationed himself in front of it. He held a brass bell and miniature hammer above his head and sounded the bell.

'The twelfth regular meeting of the New Deep Ones Society of the Pacific will come to order.' He looked around, clearly pleased with himself. Conversation had ceased and he was the target of all eyes. 'We have a distinguished guest with us tonight: Professor Marston of the University of California. If anyone can shed light on the problem of the Deep Ones, I'm sure Professor Marston can.'

Now attention shifted from the young man to Del Marston. What a farce this was turning into. Marston mulled over suitable forms of revenge against Aurelia Blenheim.

'Professor Marston,' the young man was babbling on, 'perhaps you'll be willing to address our little group.'

Marston was holding a thick sandwich in one hand and a soft drink in the other. He put them on a table and said, 'I'm afraid I'm not quite prepared for that. Maybe you'll tell me a little bit about your group, starting with your name.'

'Albert Hartley, Dr. Marston. I'm the President of the New Deep Ones Society of the Pacific. Our members are dedicated to unraveling the mystery of the Deep Ones. Hence our name.' He giggled nervously, then resumed. 'And Dr. Blenheim says that you're the leading marine geologist in the region.'

'Dr. Blenheim flatters me. But tell me about your New Deep Ones Society. Does the name refer to the fact that you're all deep thinkers?'

'Now you flatter us,' Hartley replied. They had settled onto chairs and sofas by now, the boys clustering around the girls while Albert Hartley tried to hold their attention. 'The Deep Ones (Marston could almost hear the capital letters) are strange creatures who live on the sea-bottoms of the world. People have known about them for thousands of years. They're in Greek mythology, Sumerian mythology, African mythology. And in modern times authors keep writing about them. But nowadays they have to disguise their books as fiction.'

'Why?'

Hartley looked startled. The room was silent.

Then somebody else made an ostentatious demand for the floor. Del Marston recognized the new speaker as Charlie

Einstein. The ponderous Einstein blew out a breath. 'There are people in the government who don't want us to know about the Deep Ones. People in every government. You wouldn't think that the Nazis in Germany and the Reds in Russia and the Democrats in Washington could agree on anything while they're fighting this huge war and all, but they have secret meetings in Switzerland, you know. The Japs are there, too.'

'You mean the war is a front for something else?' Marston asked. 'Cities getting blown up, soldiers dying in foxholes, aerial and naval battles, people suffering all over the world — it's all a put-up job?'

Einstein shook his head, his too-long, dirty-blond hair falling across his face. 'Oh, the war is real enough, okay. My brother is in the Army, he was at Tobruk in North Africa and was wounded and he's back in England now, in the hospital. The war is real, you bet, Dr. Marston. But the big shots who are running things still have their secret agreements. You'll see, when it ends, nothing much will change. And they really don't want us to know about the Deep Ones. Lovecraft wrote about them, too. In fact, he was writing about them even before that Czech guy, Karel Capek, wrote his book *War with the Newts*. They're everywhere. Lovecraft was a New Englander and he knew about them, they have a big base at Innsmouth, in Massachusetts.'

'But that was just fiction.' Marston tried to calm the excited youngsters. 'Foolish stories about monsters. As silly as Orson Welles' radio play about Martians. There are problems enough in this world without having to invent more.'

'Oh, no. Oh, no.' Einstein shook his head. His fleshy jowls shook with emotion. 'And another thing. There's the 1890 Paradox.'

'The what?' Marston could barely keep from laughing.

'The 1890 Paradox,' Einstein repeated. 'Karel Capek was born in 1890 in Bohemia, in what is now Czechoslovakia. Howard Phillips Lovecraft was born in Rhode Island. And Adolf Hitler was born in Linz, Austria. You can't call that a coincidence, can you?'

'Of course I can.' Marston frowned. 'Millions of people are born every year. You can pick any year out of history and find musicians, authors, politicians, scientists, generals, philosophers, all born that year. Of course it's a coincidence.'

After a moment he added, 'Besides, I'm pretty sure that Hitler was born in 1889, not 1890. Do you have an encyclopedia here? Let's look it up.'

Einstein looked pained. 'Well, 1890, 1889, those records aren't exactly reliable. It's close enough, Dr. Marston.'

Marston smiled and waited for Einstein to go on.

'Then what about their deaths? Lovecraft and Capek both wrote about the Deep Ones, both exposed their intentions, and both died within a matter of months! Explain that for me, if you can, Dr. Marston.'

'I can't explain it. There's no explaining to do. Out of all the millions of people born in 1890, I imagine that tens or hundreds of thousands would have died in — what year was it that your two writers passed on?'

'Lovecraft died in 1937, Capek in 1938.'

'And Hitler?'

'You know he's still alive. That's because the stars were right for those births in 1889 and 1890, and they were right for the two deaths in 1937 and '38. As for Hitler — he's no menace to the Deep Ones. It wouldn't surprise me if he's in league with them. Malignant beings have a long history of making alliances with humans willing to sell out their species for personal gain, like vampires offering their sort of undead immortality to their human servants. And the Deep Ones have a lot to offer their allies. Long, long life for one thing. And incredible pleasures obtained through their unspeakable rites. That's what the Deep Ones have to offer.'

'And we believe they're here, Dr. Marston.' This from Albert Hartley, taking back the center of attention. He was interrupted by a middle-aged woman who entered the room wearing a house-dress and apron. 'There's coffee and cocoa on the stove for anybody who wants them,' she announced.

Hartley looked exasperated. 'Thanks, Mom. Not right now, please.'

The woman withdrew.

'They're out in the Bay, even as we speak,' Hartley resumed. 'They have a whole city down there. When people disappear, when you hear about people jumping off the new bridge to Marin, the Deep Ones are involved in that.'

Marston frowned. It was hard to take these kids seriously but he had promised Aurelia Blenheim and he was going to do his best. 'I think the jumpers are suicides.'

'That's what you're supposed to think. The Deep Ones, they're amphibians. Lovecraft said so in his writings. They look like regular people at first. They grow up among us, they could be anybody. Then as they get older they start to show their true nature. It's called the Innsmouth Look. They start to resemble frogs or toads. Eventually they have to go back to the sea, to live with their own people.'

Marston picked up his abandoned

sandwich and took a bite. Mom Hartley made good snacks, anyway. The sandwich was spiced salami and crisp lettuce with a really sharp mustard, served on hard-crusted sourdough. Marston had a good appetite, and besides, chewing earnestly away at Mom Hartley's salami sandwich gave him an excuse not to answer young Albert Hartley's wild assertions.

Now a girl sitting surrounded by boys spoke up. 'My name is Narda Long, Dr. Marston.'

Del Marston nodded.

'We don't think that there has to be war with the Deep Ones.' Narda wore her medium brown hair in curls. Her face would be pretty, Marston decided, in a few years when she shed her baby fat. It would help her figure, too. For now, she filled her pink blouse and plaid skirt a bit more amply than she might, but in this crowd anyone young and female would get all the attention she wanted.

The room was filled with a buzz. Apparently the New Deep Ones Society was divided between those who thought they could make league with the wet folk and those who considered the amphibians the implacable enemies of land-dwellers.

'If we'd just make friends with them, I'm sure they'd leave us alone. Or even help us. Who knows what treasures there are in the sea, on the sea bottom, and we probably have things here on land that would help them.'

'That's right.' The boy sitting next to Narda Long agreed. 'We have these battles and we go shooting torpedoes around and we set off depth charges, we're probably ruining their cities. No wonder they're mad at us.'

'What can you tell us about the Deep Ones, Dr. Marston?' The only other non-hostile girl in the room, a freckled redhead, asked.

Marston shook his head. 'I think you invited the wrong person to your meeting. You need a folklorist or maybe a mystic. Somebody from the Classics Department might be good. I'm just a marine geologist. I study things like underwater volcanism and seismology, and their effect on shore structures and the way bodies of water behave. It's all pretty dry stuff.'

Nobody got the joke.

The debate went on, the let's-be-friends-with-the-frogs group versus the it's-a-fight-to-the-finish group. Finally Del Marston looked at his watch and exchanged a signal with Aurelia Blenheim.

'I'm sorry but I have to teach an early class tomorrow,' she announced. 'You know, we old folks can't stay up as late as we used to, not if we're going to go to work in the morning.'

*   *   *

'Thanks for getting us out of there,' Marston addressed Aurelia Blenheim. 'Another five minutes and I was about ready to take a couple of those young blockheads and knock their skulls together.'

Aurelia Blenheim laughed. 'They weren't that bad, Delbert. They're young, they can't help that, and a certain amount of foolish passion goes with the territory.'

'I suppose so,' Marston grumbled. 'And a couple of them even seemed moderately intelligent. The only one who seemed sensible was the young sailor — what was his name?'

'Ben Keeler. You weren't just impressed by his hero-worshipping attitude, by any chance.'

'Not in the least. Sincere and merited admiration is never misplaced and is always appreciated.'

'What a lovely aphorism.' Aurelia Blenheim leaned forward and switched on the Cord's radio. The phaeton had cleared the Bay Bridge, the structural steel and giant cables of which would have interfered with reception. A late-night broadcaster was rhapsodizing about the progress of General Clark's forces in Italy and the successes of Admiral Nimitz's fleet against the Japanese. The announcer must have been local because he went on to talk about Nimitz's pre-war connection with the University of California in Berkeley.

When the news broadcast ended Marston switched to a station playing a Mozart clarinet piece. 'You don't really think those kids have something, do you?'

he asked his companion.

'I try to keep an open mind.'

Marston asked, not for the first time, how his friend had first encountered the New Deep Ones. As usual she referred to a vague relationship between herself and Mrs. Hartley. 'We went to school together a million years ago. I was in her wedding. Poor Walter, her husband, was on a sub that went down in the Pacific. She carries on and I try to keep her spirits up.'

'And you really do have a class in the morning,' Marston commented. He drove through Berkeley, dropped her at her home on Garber Street and returned to his home on Brookside Drive.

He refused further invitations to attend meetings of the New Deep Ones. His feet were bothering him and walking had become difficult and uncomfortable if not downright painful. And he was having problems with his jaw and teeth. He consulted his dentist and his medical doctor alternately. Each reported that he could find no source for Marston's difficulties and referred him to the other.

Marston worked at his office on

campus, solving problems brought to him from local naval installations. He reduced his social schedule until he was a near recluse, moving between his bachelor's bungalow and his office on the university campus. He met requests for his company with increasingly abrasive refusals until the day he realized he was excluded from faculty cocktail parties and all but the most compulsory of campus events.

The conversation he had in part overheard, in part contributed to, at the meeting of the New Deep Ones preyed on his mind. Several times he sought out Aurelia Blenheim, by now not only his longest-enduring acquaintance but virtually his only friend. Over a cup of coffee or a glass of wine he queried her about Selena Hartley, young Albert's mother. At least Aurelia Blenheim had revealed her friend's first name.

Her maiden name had been Curwen. She was a native San Franciscan, descended from the founder of Curwen Heights. She had married Walter at the height of the tumultuous Roaring Twenties and had struggled at his side through the years of the Depression to preserve their relationship and to keep the old house, built by the original Eben Curwen in the previous century, in the family. Beyond that, Aurelia Blenheim had no information to share with Delbert Marston.

★　★　★

Naval Intelligence had ferreted out Japanese plans to send submarines against the West Coast of the United States. To Marston this made no sense. Earlier in the war, after the Japanese had decimated the US Pacific Fleet at Pearl Harbor and had conquered the Philippines and Wake Island, it would have made sense. But the Japanese were being forced back by General MacArthur's island hopping campaign and General LeMay's fire-bombing of the home islands.

An anti-submarine net had been strung across the Golden Gate in 1942, when a direct attack by Admiral Yamamoto's forces seemed imminent. The attack had never come, but the Navy had been spooked by their intelligence and Marston was called on to help design a new and improved underwater defense line. Knowing the Navy, the war would be over before the new defenses were built and the defenses would be outdated before another war could make them useful, but Marston was not one to shirk his duty.

He spent his days touring the Bay and the Golden Gate in naval motor launches, alternating the excursions with long days at the desk calculator and the drawing board. His nights he spent in his living room, looking out over Brookside Drive, listening to music, and drinking scotch whiskey. It was almost impossible to find good single malt nowadays, far more difficult than it had been during the laughably ineffective Prohibition of Marston's youth. He shuddered at the thought of having to switch to blended swill.

As walking became increasingly painful he spent more hours in the University pool. Even sitting in an easy chair or lying in bed he had to deal with discomfort, and the ongoing changes in his jaw and teeth made eating a nasty chore. He was losing his teeth one by one, and new ones were emerging in their place. He'd heard of people getting a third set of teeth, it was a rare but not-unknown phenomenon. His own new teeth were triangular in shape and razor-sharp. Only when he had slipped into the waters of the pool did the pain in his extremities ease, and even his mouth felt less discomfort.

Yet he was drawing unwelcome glances in the changing area at the pool. He altered his routine, suiting up at home and wearing baggy clothing over his trunks until he reached the locker room. There he would doff his outer costume and plunge into the water, staying beneath the surface as long as he could before rising for air. As time passed he found himself able to stay under for longer periods. He ascribed this to the practice of almost daily swims.

One day he stayed under for a period that must have set his personal record. When he surfaced he was the center of attention. One of the other swimmers muttered, 'Say, you must have been down there for five or six minutes. How do you do that?'

Marston growled an answer, then hastened to his locker, pulled his baggy clothing on over his wet body and dripping suit, and headed for home.

That night he drove to the Berkeley Marina. He parked his Cord, looked around and ascertained that he was alone. He walked to the water's edge, disrobed, and slipped into the Bay. The water was icy but somehow it eased the now-constant ache in his legs and feet. His hands, too, seemed to be changing their shape in some small, subtle way. They were uncomfortable, as well. He wondered if he was developing arthritis.

He swam out toward Angel Island. He had no way of knowing just how far he had gone or how long he had remained submerged, but he felt that it must have been fifteen or twenty minutes. He broke surface and realized that he was not out of breath. In fact, he had to force himself to inhale the fog-drenched night air. His neck itched and he rubbed it with his hands, feeling horizontal ridges of muscle that he had never noticed before.

He looked around, searching for landmarks, but the enforced wartime blackout precluded the use of bright lights in the cities that lined San Francisco Bay. He made out the silhouette of the Bay Bridge against the sky, then that of the Golden Gate Bridge. He turned in the water, recognizing the forbidding fortifications of Alcatraz. Without inhaling again he ducked beneath the surface and swam back toward the Berkeley shoreline. In time he waded from the cold, brackish waters of the Bay. By contrast, the night air felt warm against his body. He shook like a dog to rid himself of water, pulled on his clothing, and drove home.

In the Brookside Drive cottage he drew a polished captain's chair to an open window. Through the window he could hear the soft gurgle of the nearby stream that gave the thoroughfare its name. Odd, Marston thought, that he had never noticed this before. The sound brought with it a melancholy, pleasant feeling. He thought of putting a record on the turntable, had even selected Handel's *Music for the Royal Fireworks*, and pouring himself a scotch while he listened to the recording, but instead brought a pillow from his bedroom and placed it on the living room carpet.

He lay down in darkness and closed his eyes, letting the sound of the stream fill his consciousness. He fell asleep and dreamed of dark waters, strange creatures and ancient cities beneath the sea. He awoke the following morning and staggered to the mirror in his bedroom. He brushed water from his hair.

By the end of May, in normal times, the university's spring semester would have ended and the students departed, leaving Berkeley a quiet suburb of Oakland instead of the bustling community of scholars it became during the academic year. But in wartime the military had set up accelerated programs for the education of junior officers, and the University of California was on a year-round schedule.

Delbert Marston's assignments from

his naval superiors had changed as well. The computations and design of the antisubmarine defenses were completed and construction was well under way. The data provided to Marston now was peculiar and the requested analytical reports were more peculiar than ever. In Europe the long-anticipated cross-channel invasion had taken place and Allied forces were pushing the Wehrmacht back toward Germany. In the Pacific, Japanese troops were resisting with fanatical dedication, whole units dying to the last soldier rather than raise the flag of surrender.

But as the Office of War Information reminded the American public, the conflict was far from over. The Germans had developed flying bombs and rocket weapons and were using them against Allied forces in France and Belgium, and sending them to wreak havoc in England. If they could develop longer-range models, even the US would be in danger. A Nazi super-scientist named Heisenberg was rumored to be developing a weapon of unprecedented power that could be delivered to New York by a jet-propelled flying wing bomber. The whole thing seemed like a scenario from a Fritz Lang movie.

Still, Marston made his way to his office each morning, laboring on feet that sent agony lancing up his increasingly deformed legs. Once at work he found it hard even to hold a pencil, relying on an assistant to take dictation rather than try to write up his own notes. He seldom spoke with anyone save his naval superiors and assistants.

His only pleasures were his solitary, nocturnal excursions beneath the surface of the Bay. He no longer bothered with the fiction of breathing air once he entered the Bay, relying on water inhaled through his now wide mouth and expelled through the gill slits in his neck once his body had extracted its oxygen content.

He saw shapes beneath the water now, sometimes dark, sometimes sickly luminescent. At first he avoided them, then he began to pursue them. He couldn't make out their shapes well, either, although as time passed he began to develop more acute vision in the dark medium. From time to time one of the shapes would swim toward him, then flash aside when he reached out to touch it.

One night he found one of the creatures drifting aimlessly a few feet beneath the surface. He swam to it and saw that it was more or less human in shape but clearly not human. He reached for it and it did not flash away. Once he grasped it he realized that it was dead, its flesh horribly torn as if it had been caught in the propeller of a passing ship. Even as he studied the strange cadaver two more shapes flashed into sight and snatched it from his grasp, moving first out of his reach and then out of his sight.

But he had touched the remains. The flesh was white and stringy, the skin as smooth and slick as that of a giant frog.

Despite the changes he was undergoing he managed to maintain the pretense of normality, taking his meals, filling his Cord Phaeton with precious, rationed gasoline, sending his laundry out to be done, keeping his modest lodgings in order.

Late one Saturday afternoon he nearly collided with Aurelia Blenheim while pushing a shopping cart in the aisle of the grocery store nearest his home. He was shocked at her haggard appearance. How long had it been since their last meeting? How could she have aged so badly? He thought of his own changed appearance and wondered if he looked as worrisome to Aurelia as she to him.

The expression on Aurelia Blenheim's face showed shock and deep concern. 'Delbert,' the elderly woman exclaimed, 'are you all right?'

'Of course I am.'

'But you look so — are you certain?'

'Yes,' he growled. He should have turned and left the store the instant he spotted Blenheim, but he had failed to act and now he was caught. 'I'm just a little tired,' he explained. 'Very tired, in fact. The war. So much work.'

'I'm coming to your house,' Blenheim asserted. 'I'm going to make dinner for you. You're not taking care of yourself.

You're headed for the hospital if you don't get yourself together. You should be ashamed!'

When they reached Marston's cottage he turned his key in the door lock and stood aside to let Aurelia Blenheim enter first. Marston carried the bag of groceries Blenheim had helped him select. She had even loaned him a few ration stamps and tokens to complete his purchase.

The selection of foodstuffs was far more extensive than the Spartan diet Marston had been living on in recent months. In fact he occasionally supplemented his nourishment during his nocturnal swims in the Bay. That body was densely populated with marine species that throve in its cold, brackish waters. Marston became ravenous when he came upon the abalone, eels, crabs, clams and small octopods that lurked in the silted seabed. When he came upon one he would devour it raw, fresh, and sometimes living. His new teeth could pierce the shell of a living crab as if it were paper.

Just inside the doorway Aurelia Blenheim bent over and picked up a buff-colored envelope. 'Here's a telegram for you, Delbert.'

He took the envelope from her and opened it. The message was typed in capital letters on strips of buff paper and glued to the message form. The telegram came from a Captain Kinne, commanding officer of the Naval Weapons Station at Port Chicago, a village on the shore of Suisun Bay, an extension of San Francisco Bay fed by the Sacramento River.

The message itself was terse. It directed Marston to report to the commanding officer's headquarters first thing Monday morning. In traditional naval fashion Marston was told to show up at or about 0600 hours, on or about 3 July 1944. Marston had never heard of anyone in the Navy arriving after the designated time and date with the excuse that he had arrived 'about' the indicated time.

Aurelia Blenheim steered Marston into an easy chair and carried the bag of groceries into his kitchen. She had visited the Brookside Drive cottage before, although months had passed since her last visit. Marston put some light music on the turntable, an RCA Red Seal twelve-inch recording of *Vltava* by the tragic Bohemian madman Bedrich Smetana.

With astonishing speed Blenheim produced a tempting bouillabaisse. The odor coming from the kitchen was mouthwatering and the flavor of the marine stew proved delicious. The only problem, for Marston, was that everything seemed overdone. He would have preferred to consume the aquatic creatures uncooked.

After dinner they relaxed in Marston's living room with glasses of pre-war brandy. Jokingly, Aurelia Blenheim asked why Marston's mother hadn't taught him to take better care of himself. When he reacted to the question with frowning silence the older woman set down her glass and took his free hand between both of hers. 'I'm sorry. I didn't mean to upset you.'

Marston drew away. Of late his arthritis had become worse. The last joints of his fingers and toes had curled downwards and his finger-and toenails seemed to be turning into claws. He worked to keep them trimmed but they grew back rapidly. The small triangles of flesh between the bases of his digits were growing, also, a change that proved helpful in water but embarrassing in public.

Desperate to draw attention away from his increasing physical abnormalities, Marston said, 'No, I'm afraid she didn't.'

Blenheim frowned, 'Who didn't what?'

'My mother. She never taught me to take care of myself. She never taught me anything. I never knew her. My father told me that she loved to swim. They lived in Chicago and she would swim in Lake Michigan all year round. She joined a group, they called themselves the Polar Bear Club, and they would plunge into the lake every New Year's Day, no matter how cold it was, even if it was snowing. But that was just a stunt. They used to get their picture in the Chicago *Times* and the *Tribune* and the *Sun*. But Mother took it all very seriously. The photographers loved her, she was the only female Polar Bear.'

He took a deep draught of golden liqueur.

'She was an immigrant,' he resumed. 'I never knew where she was born. Father just said it was a cold country. I was born on December 25, you know,' he changed the subject. 'I was a Christmas baby.' He said it with bitterness. 'Father brought Mother and me home from the hospital on New Year's Eve. The next day Mother insisted on her annual plunge with the other Polar Bears. They used to run out into the lake, throw themselves into the surf, frisk for a few minutes and then come running back out of the water. But Mother swam out. Snow was falling, Father told me, and visibility was poor. Mother just swam out into the lake. They sent search parties after her but they never found her.'

'I'm so sorry,' Aurelia Blenheim said. She started again to reach for his hand, then drew back, avoiding a repetition of his previous withdrawal. After a moment she said, 'Did your father ever remarry?'

Marston shook his head. 'He raised me

alone, as best he could, until he was gunned down when I was six. I had no other relatives and I wound up bouncing from one orphanage to another until I went out on my own.'

'But you've made such a success of yourself, Delbert. I never knew about your childhood. How sad. But look at you now, a tenured professor, a respected member of the community. I'm so proud of you, and you should be proud of yourself.'

She insisted on clearing the dishes and cleaning up Marston's kitchen. She returned to the living room and said, 'You know I live nearby. I'll just walk home, it's such a warm evening. Please promise me you'll take better care of yourself. And let me know how things work out at Port Chicago. As much as the Navy lets you tell me, of course.'

He stood on his lawn and watched until she disappeared. He returned to his house and filled another snifter of brandy, then sipped until it was gone. The summer evening was long and he was in agony by the time full darkness descended. Then he left the house and drove to the marina. He parked, disrobed at the water's edge and slipped into the Bay.

Monday morning he rose early and drove to Port Chicago. The naval base consisted mainly of warehouses and barracks. A railroad spur ran onto a pier that extended into the Bay. Even at this early hour he could see crews of black stevedores in navy fatigues working to move munitions from railroad cars to the hold of a ship moored to the side of the pier. The stevedores were supervised by white men in officers' uniforms.

A guard had demanded to see Marston's identification and the telegram summoning him to the base. Once satisfied, the guard directed Marston to the headquarters building, a wood-frame structure badly in need of fresh paint. Once inside he was escorted by a smartly-uniformed WAVE into the commander's office.

Captain Kinne looked as if he had stepped out of a bandbox. Every crease in his uniform was knife-sharp, every button glistened.

Marston of course wore civilian garb, the academic uniform of tweed jacket, flannel slacks and button-down shirt. He had replaced his customary striped necktie with a scarf that concealed his gill-slits and added a pair of oversized dark glasses. He stood in front of Captain Kinne's desk wondering whether he was expected to salute or shake hands. The WAVE introduced him and Kinne looked up at him. 'You're Marston, eh?'

He said, 'I am.'

'All right, I just wanted to get a look at you. Tell a lot about a man with one look. You'll do. What happened to your hands, Marston? Some kind of tropical disease? Jungle rot?'

Marston started to answer but Kinne went on.

'Jaspers,' he addressed the WAVE, 'take Mr. Marston down the hall. Give him to Keeler.' He turned back to Marston and nodded curtly. 'Go with Jaspers. Keeler will tell you what to do. Thanks for coming.'

The WAVE, obviously Jaspers, led

Marston to another office. She halted and knocked at the door, then turned the knob and opened the door a few inches. 'Mr. Marston is here, sir.'

She gestured and Marston stepped past her into the office. He heard Jaspers close the door behind him. He found himself in a smaller office now, surrounded by charts and manuals. The man who stood up to greet him wore a set of summer khakis with the twin tracks of a Navy lieutenant on the collar.

'A real pleasure to see you again, Dr. Marston. After that little party in Curwen Heights I was afraid you wouldn't want anything to do with us.'

'Ben Keeler?' Marston said. 'You've certainly risen fast. You were a junior petty officer the last time I saw you.'

Keeler grinned. 'Petty Officer Third Ben Keeler, Lieutenant Benjamin Keeler, same fellow. ONI put me in that EM's uniform to check out the New Deep Ones Society. They were pretty worried at one point, those kids were getting too close to the truth and Naval Intelligence wanted them steered off. That was my job. I still attend their meetings, by the way. If you ever want to come by again, I'd love some moral support. Just don't blow my cover.'

'All right,' Marston smiled. 'I wouldn't want to get you in trouble with Naval Intelligence.'

'And they're just a bunch of harmless eccentrics, you know,' Keeler added. He walked around the desk and put his arm on Marston's shoulders. 'Take a walk with me, Dr. Marston. There are some things you need to see, and then some questions I'll want to ask you.'

Marston acceded, determined not to show the pain that he knew he was in for. At Keeler's side he made his way along the pier. A freighter stood in the middle of Suisun Bay, black smoke pouring from its stacks. It would clear the Golden Gate before noon, Marston knew, en route to the soldiers and marines fighting the Japanese in the Pacific. An empty ship had already taken the place of the freighter on one side of the pier, while another, opposite it, received pallets and crates of munitions.

As they moved past work gangs Keeler took salutes from ensigns and petty officers supervising the stevedores. The latter continued to work as Marston and Keeler passed.

At the end of the pier they halted. A breeze had kicked up and the surface of Suisun Bay had turned choppy.

Marston gestured back toward the work gangs they had passed. 'All of the stevedores are black, all of the officers are white,' he commented. The question was implicit.

'Navy policy,' Keeler shrugged. 'Not very long ago the Navy was trying to get rid of all its Negroes, even though they were just mess-men and laundry workers. Filipinos make better workers. But there's too much pressure from Washington, finally the service gave in. And these colored stevedores are pretty good, as long as you keep a close eye on them.'

They turned to face the buildings of Port Chicago. 'What we're concerned about, Del, is a very special cargo that we're going to ship out this month.'

Marston nodded, then waited for

Keeler to continue.

'It's a very special bomb. It's coming in by train next week, and Captain Kinne wanted to get your help in handling it.'

Marston shook his head. 'What do I know about bombs?'

'Oh, we have plenty of people who know about bombs,' Keeler grinned. 'We need somebody who knows hydrology and submarine geology to keep this baby safe.'

'What is it, something bigger than the ones LeMay is dropping on Japan? The closer we get to the home islands, the easier it's going to be to hit 'em.'

'No,' Keeler shook his head. 'This is something different. Look, everybody knows that we're close to finishing off the European war. Ike took a big risk with the Normandy landings but that was a big success and Patton and Montgomery are rolling through France. Italy's out of the game. And the Russians are closing in on the Nazis from the East. It's just a matter of time now.'

'And in the Pacific, too, don't you agree, Benjamin?'

'But we're taking terrible losses. The President is up for reelection this November and those casualties are going to hurt him. He's put pressure on the War Department and the Navy Department to give him this bigger, better bomb. We figure once we drop a couple of these babies on Japan, maybe one on Tokyo and one on Kobe, even the fanatical Nips will cave in. Washington doesn't want to have to invade the home islands, don't you see. That's what this is all about, Del.'

There was a moment of silence as a zephyr swept in from the Bay, bringing the smell of brine and brackish waters with it. Then the wind shifted and the clatter of tools, the sound of voices, the roar of donkey engines came to them from the ships and the railroad cars.

'And there's another thing,' Keeler added. 'You know Uncle Sam didn't much care for the Bolshies when they first took over Russia twenty-five years ago. President Wilson even sent some troops over there. The government doesn't like to talk about that any more now that Joe Stalin is our buddy but you know we took sides in their civil war and we picked a loser.'

'That was a long time ago,' Marston put in.

The combination of the choppy Bay and the increasingly brisk breeze whipped up a spray of salt-flavored water that pelted onto the pier and onto Keeler and Marston. Keeler pulled a bandanna from his uniform trousers pocket and wiped his face, frowning. Marston licked his lips. He felt hugely refreshed.

'The US wouldn't even recognize the new government in Russia until Roosevelt came in, and there are still a lot of powerful men in Washington who don't trust Stalin and his gang. They want to get this new bomb and use it before the war is over as a warning to the Reds not to get too big for their britches.'

He hooked his arm through Marston's and the two men strolled back along the pier, returning finally to Keeler's office. Keeler said, 'Will you get to work on this, Del? Captain Kinne has already worked it out with his counterparts, you'll be excused from your other duties until the special bomb is safely out on the ocean, on its way to a bomber base in the islands. We need your analysis and your recommendations about the seabed and waters from here to the Farralons. And we need your report before that ship moves. The bomb is coming in next week, and we need to get it out of here on the *Quinalt Victory*. Our stevedores will be working on the *Bryan* most of the time, that will serve as cover for the bomb going out on the *Quinalt*.'

Keeler opened a safe and extracted a pass for Marston. 'This will get you anywhere on the base,' he said. 'Guard it, Del, it could be dangerous if it got away from you.'

Marston accepted the pass, slipped it into his pocket and left.

He spent the next few days alternating between Port Chicago and the University campus in Berkeley, studying the physical layout at Suisun Bay and existing charts and studies of the area. He could hardly hold himself back from examining the seabed in person, but he resisted the temptation until he felt ready.

Then he drove from Berkeley to Port Chicago after dark, parked the Cord, and walked out to the pier. The work here went on around the clock, seven days a week. There was no way he could use the pier without being observed, so he informed the young officer supervising the loading work of his intentions.

At the end of the pier he left his clothing, climbed down a ladder, and slipped into the water.

The Bay water was cold and dark and as it welcomed him he felt the aches leave his body and limbs. He had always been a strong swimmer; now, the webbing between his fingers and between his toes turned him into a virtual amphibian. His eyes, too, had developed a sensitivity that permitted him to maneuver in the dark, brackish water.

He spotted a huge dark-green crab scuttling toward a large rock on the seabed. The creature didn't have a chance. Marston's new, powerful jaw and strong, triangular teeth crunched through its shell. The living meat was sweet and the juices of the crab were more delicious than the finest liquor.

Marston saw human-like forms swimming nearby and pursued them. Ever since his encounter with the dead creature he had wondered about these beings. They might be a species of giant batrachian hitherto unknown to science, far larger than any recorded frog or toad; perhaps they were survivors of a species of amphibian that had evolved eons ago only to disappear from most of the world.

He swam after them and they permitted him to approach them but not to establish direct contact. They swam with the current created by the waters of the Sacramento River as it emptied into Suisun Bay. They looked back from time to time as if to encourage Marston to follow them, but the speed and stamina with which they swam far exceeded even his enhanced abilities.

Finally he gave up and swam back toward the loading pier and the two ships at Port Chicago.

He climbed the ladder, then drew himself onto the pier. The young ensign he had spoken with earlier greeted him with a shake of his head. 'I was getting pretty worried,' the ensign said. 'Do you know how long you were gone, sir? And do you realize how cold the Bay is, and how tricky the currents can be?'

Marston didn't feel like talking with this youngster but he managed a few polite words. Yes, he knew exactly what he was doing, he had never been in danger, there was nothing to worry about but he appreciated the ensign's concern.

During the brief conversation he had been pulling his clothing back on. He had purchased new shoes, as wide as he could find, to accommodate his newly altered feet. Even so, it was fiercely painful to force his feet into them.

He repeated his activities each night. The underwater creatures gradually grew accustomed to him, permitting him to approach ever more closely, permitting him to accompany them farther and farther from Port Chicago. It was clear to Marston that they communicated with one another, mainly by means of subtle gestures made with their broad, webbed, clawed hands. Marston inferred that they had a language as sophisticated and complex as any spoken by land-dwellers.

Now that he was affiliated with the Port Chicago base Marston had discontinued all contacts with his former associates in Berkeley. He did not worry about running into Aurelia Blenheim at the grocery as he now relied entirely on a diet of creatures he encountered during his nocturnal explorations of the Bay's waters.

He maintained a relationship with Lieutenant Keeler and through him with Captain Kinne, furnishing reports and recommendations as required of him. He resented every meeting he had to attend, every conversation he had to conduct; in fact, he found himself living for his submarine excursions and suffering through each hour he spent walking on land, breathing with his gradually atrophying lungs instead of his gills.

On Friday, July 14, Keeler demanded that Marston attend a meeting with Captain Kinne. Also present were two high-ranking officers, one from the Navy and the other from the Army, the latter with Army Air Force insignia on his uniform blouse, and the commanders of the stevedoring gangs.

Captain Kinne's WAVE secretary, Jaspers, ushered Marston into the commanding officer's area. When the meeting participants were assembled they were joined by a pair of armed shore patrolmen and the doors securely locked.

'The bomb will arrive in forty-eight hours,' the army officer announced. A major general's paired silver stars glittered on his uniform shoulders. 'We will deliver it to the loading pier, then we need a sign-off from the Navy and our job is finished.'

'And ours begins,' the naval officer took over. His uniform sleeves bore the broad gold stripes of a rear admiral. 'Captain Kinne, are your men ready to get the bomb stowed in *Quinalt Victory* Monday evening? ONI insists that we do the loading at night, but it must be finished in time to catch the late tide out of the Golden Gate.' The admiral cast a sharp look at Marston. 'Dr. Marston has provided all the information we'll need to get *Quinalt Victory* safely out of the Bay and on her way by midnight?'

The utterance was worded as a statement but spoken as a question.

'We have everything, sir,' Keeler furnished.

'All right. Let's go over the complete plan again,' the admiral growled. 'There must be no slip-ups, I can't emphasize that too much.'

They spent the rest of the day going over the details of unloading the special bomb from its railroad car and loading it into the hold of the *Quinalt Victory* without a hitch. A squad of white-jacketed mess-men served coffee and rolls at midmorning and a full meal at noon. No one left the meeting for any reason. Marston was able to pass up the coffee and rolls but by lunch time he was forced to consume a few sips of beverage and half a sandwich. This disgusted him.

When the meeting ended he drove into Port Chicago. He had seen the town fleetingly each day but today for the first time he parked his Cord and walked through the town. He found a motion picture theater and purchased a ticket. They were running a long program, the dramatic film *Lifeboat* with Tallulah Bankhead and Canada Lee, the light-weight *Bathing Beauty* with Esther Williams, a newsreel and a chapter of 'Crash' Corrigan's old serial, *Undersea Kingdom*.

Once inside he settled into a seat and unlaced his shoes, finding a modicum of relief for his aching feet. He leaned back and studied the neon-ringed clock mounted high on one wall of the auditorium. Most of the patrons were servicemen in uniform, whiling away their off-duty hours. None of them were black. Negroes were excluded from the theater and from the town's plain restaurants. They had to find their own entertainment, or make it.

Marston ignored the images on the screen and closed his eyes. Images of undersea life swam through his mind, the peace and serenity of the submarine world contrasting with the pain and violence that dominated the world of the land-dwellers.

After a while he opened his eyes and glanced at the illuminated clock-face. Even in the long July evening, darkness would have fallen by now.

He drove back to the naval base, showed his pass to the gate-guard, and parked as near to the water's edge as he could. He carefully locked the Cord and walked to the base of the pier. A special guard had been placed there, and even Marston's special pass could not gain him access to the pier.

Instead he walked back to his car, unlocked the door and climbed inside. He disrobed, left the car again, and walked undiscovered to the edge of the Bay. He slipped into the Bay and swam away from the shore.

He made his way to the cold, flowing water that he knew came from the Sacramento River. The river water had less flavor than the Bay water. With a start Marston realized that he had never experienced the richness of the Pacific. He turned to swim with the current. His anticipation of the new experience filled him with an almost sexual excitement.

When he reached the submarine net at the mouth of San Francisco Bay he paused briefly, then pulled himself through it into the ocean. He was terrified but soon calmed himself. He had undergone a rite of passage, he felt, had experienced a sea change. He would explore farther in later days, he decided, but for now he felt emotionally drained and physically exhausted.

He turned and began the long swim back to Suisun Bay.

He had seen fewer of the human-like creatures than usual on this night, but as he approached Port Chicago they became more numerous. He was beginning to learn their language and felt eager to converse with them, find out who or what they were, but they kept their distance from him this night, and instead of joining them he continued on his solitary way.

In time he recognized the submerged landmarks that told him he was at his destination. He had been swimming along the sea bottom, insulated by fathoms of brackish water from the world of men, immune from the noisome companionship of air breathers and land dwellers. He rose slowly toward the top of the water. He was shocked as he breached to realize that he had spent the entire night under water. The brilliant sun now blasted down from a bright blue sky.

He made his way to his Cord, drove home and slept around the clock. He awoke Sunday morning and spent the day in seclusion, sustaining himself with alcohol and music. After dark he made his way to the nearby stream and stood in it, letting its waters soothe his feet. He went home and slept, dreaming once more of an undersea city, and rose late on Monday. He hadn't realized how far he had swum on Friday night, or how exhausted the effort had left him. Still, the experience had been an exhilarating one and he looked forward to spending even more time beneath the surface, to travelling farther into the ocean.

When he reached Port Chicago on Monday the transfer of the bomb from railroad freight car to the hold of *Quinalt Victory* was well under way. Marston's expertise had been of immense value, he would be told. He encountered Captain Kinne himself on the pier and the usually stern Kinne recognized him and thanked him for his assistance.

Powerful electric vapor-lights had been rigged to illuminate the operation once the sun had set and their peculiar glare gave the faces of the men on the pier a ghostly look.

Marston walked to the end of the pier. When he turned back toward the center of activity he saw that all eyes were fixed on the delicate work at the *Quinalt Victory*. He checked his wristwatch and saw that it was ten o'clock. Bright moonlight was reflected off the surface of the Bay.

Instead of climbing down the ladder to the water's surface, Marston left his clothing in its usual neat pile, stood on the edge of the pier, and dived into the Bay. He swam to the seabed, taking delicious water in and passing it through his gills, letting his eyes grow accustomed to the faint phosphorescence that provided illumination in this world.

He turned to observe the hull of the *Quinalt Victory*. He was astonished at the number of human-like forms moving around the ship, gesturing meaningfully to one another, attaching something, something to the metal hull of the *Quinalt Victory*.

Marston swam toward the ship, curious as to what the creatures were doing. This was the first time he had seen them using anything that looked like machinery. As he drew closer several of the creatures turned and swam toward him. As they approached he realized that they were like him in every way. The wide mouth and triangular teeth, the splayed limbs, the webbed hands and feet, the hooked claws, the oversized eyes and flattened noses.

How had he managed to pass among men until now? How had his alienness gone undetected? The scarf and dark glasses had helped but surely he would be caught out soon if he tried to continue his masquerade as human. He raised a hand and gestured, showing these aquatic beings that he was one of them, telling them in their own language, a language

which he was just beginning to compre-
hend, that he was not a human, not a
land-dweller.

He was not the enemy.

He was shocked by a brilliant flash
from the *Quinalt Victory*, a glare that
seemed as bright as the sun. Marston felt
a shock wave, felt its unimaginable,
crushing pressure as it reached him.
Then, even before he could react, there
was a second flash, this one brighter than
a thousand suns, and a second shock
wave infinitely greater than the first. But
he felt it for only the most fleeting of
moments, and then he felt nothing more.

* * *

Historic Note

At 10:20 PM, Monday, July 17, 1944, a
huge explosion occurred at Port Chicago,
California. Two ships were moored at the
loading pier of the naval station there.
The *E.A.Bryan* was fully loaded and
ready to leave for the Pacific theater of
operations with a huge cargo of high

explosives and military equipment. The *Quinalt Victory*, a brand new vessel built at the Kaiser Shipyard in nearby Richmond, California, was preparing to take on its own cargo.

Some three hundred and twenty individuals were killed in the explosion, most of them African-American stevedores. An additional four hundred persons were injured. A common form of injury was blindness caused by flying splinters of window-glass in naval barracks. The main explosion was preceded by a rumble or smaller explosion, reports differing, which drew many off-duty stevedores to the windows to see what had caused the sound.

The brilliant flash, the roar of the explosion, and the shaking of the earth that resulted, were seen, heard, and felt as far away as the cities of Berkeley, Oakland, and San Francisco.

The *Bryan*, the *Quinalt Victory*, the loading pier, the railroad spur running along the pier, and the ammunition train that was parked on the pier at the time, were all totally destroyed. The town of Port Chicago was obliterated and a visitor to its site today will find only a few forlorn street markers to show where once a community thrived.

While official statements about the disaster aver only to the high explosives which had been loaded in the *E.A.Bryan*, critics in later years suggested that the explosion was nuclear in nature. In the summer of 1944 the atomic bomb was top secret and the very existence of the Manhattan Project was shrouded in layers of security. But once the bomb was dropped on Hiroshima and Nagasaki, speculation began that more than dynamite had been involved in the Port Chicago disaster.

If the Port Chicago explosion was indeed nuclear in nature, further speculation is divided between those who believe the explosion was accidental in origin, or was in fact a test by the United States government to measure the effects of a nuclear bomb. Certainly the weapons base at Port Chicago would have made a fine test subject, with ships, a railroad spur, temporary and permanent buildings, and many hundreds of expendable human subjects.

Perhaps the Port Chicago explosion was a nuclear accident. If so, it represented a major setback to the American nuclear weapons project. The successful Alamogordo test did not take place until July 16, 1945, one day short of a year after the Port Chicago explosion. Nuclear weapons were exploded in the air over Hiroshima and Nagasaki the following month, bringing about the end of the Second World War and providing an object lesson for Josef Stalin.

Where the Port Chicago naval weapons depot once stood, there is now the Concord Naval Weapons Station, a major loading area for the United States Pacific Fleet. The storage of nuclear weapons in barrow-like bunkers at the naval weapons station, while not officially acknowledged by the US government, is one of the most ill-kept secrets of our era.